THE NEW RECRUIT

Doolin and Bitter Creek were sitting at their usual table at the Ransom and Murray Saloon. Doolin had a shot of whiskey in front of him.

"This here's Bill Dalton," I said.

My brother offered his hand, but Doolin just nodded. Bitter Creek touched a finger to the brim of his hat.

We sat down with them.

Doolin looked Bill up and down and took a sip of his whiskey. "I thought you were a senator or some other kind of high-and-mighty politician out yonder in California," he said.

"Well, I did have political ambitions," Bill said. "But the thing was, after my brothers were wrongly accused of robbing so many banks and trains, everything went sour for me. Folks didn't want a politician with the last name of Dalton. After Coffeyville, it was hopeless."

"So what are you doing in the Territory?" Doolin asked.

"I want to join up."

"With the Wild Bunch?"

"Yes, sir."

"What in hell for?" I asked.

"Gold and glory," he said. "And revenge."

Also by Max McCoy

THE SIXTH RIDER
SONS OF FIRE

THE WILD RIDER

Max McCoy

BANTAM BOOKS
NEW YORK • TORONTO • LONDON • SYDNEY • AUCKLAND

THE WILD RIDER
A Bantam Domain Book / June 1995

ISBN 0-553-56444-7

Published simultaneously in the United States and Canada

Bantam Books are published by Bantam Books, a division of Bantam
Doubleday Dell Publishing Group, Inc. Its trademark, consisting of the
words "Bantam Books" and the portrayal of a rooster, is Registered in
U.S. Patent and Trademark Office and in other countries. Marca Reg-
istrada. Bantam Books, 1540 Broadway, New York, New York 10036.

PRINTED IN THE UNITED STATES OF AMERICA

OPM   0 9 8 7 6 5 4 3 2 1

For Krista,
who saw it in the cards

The biggest fool on earth is the one who thinks he can beat the law, that crime can be made to pay. It never paid and it never will and that was the one big lesson of the Coffeyville raid.

—*Emmett Dalton*

I've labored long and hard for bread
For honor and for riches
But on my corns too long you've tread
You fine-haired· Sons of Bitches.

—*Black Bart, Po8*

Ingalls, Oklahoma Territory
September 1, 1893

FIRST STREET

A. LIGHT, BLACKSMITH

HOSTETLER-PIERCE LIVERY

VAUGHN SALOON

Draw

Grove

THOMAS RESTAURANT

ASH STREET

SADIE COMLEY'S

PERRY DRY GOODS

WALNUT STREET

PUBLIC WELL

O.K. HOTEL

PICKERING HOME

SECOND STREET

RANSOM & MURRAY SALOON

CALL'S PHARMACY

OAK STREET

RANSOM LIVERY

DOC SELPH'S

Fence

RANSOM HOME

THIRD STREET

Draw

©RON TOELKE 1995

One

Icrossed into Kansas from the Nations along about midnight, judging by the stars that wheel around the pole. It was a cold night and Cimarron's breath issued in great locomotive bursts from his nostrils. There was an orange smudge in the sky over Coffeyville, thrown by the bonfire the authorities had built in the middle of the town plaza. I knew that scores of grim-faced men with Winchesters would be standing watch, waiting to finish off what was left of the Dalton Gang, but I was intent on avoiding the plaza—this trip to Coffeyville was only going to take me as far as Elmwood Cemetery, to visit the graves of my brothers before I attended to some business in Caney.

I tied Cimarron in the timber along the Verdigris River and I went the rest of the way on foot, keeping to the shadows and stopping every hundred yards or so to make sure that nobody was about. I had left my spurs behind, but even the sound of my footsteps seemed uncommon loud in the stillness, so I sat down in the road and pulled off my boots. I made the last quarter mile to the cemetery in my stocking feet, with my teeth chattering from the cold and the boots tucked under my left elbow so as to leave my shooting hand free.

Not that I was looking for trouble, but I *was* in Coffeyville, and people there have a tendency to use Daltons to sift lead. Less than a month had passed since the Dalton raid of Saturday, October 5, 1892—folks were already citing the full historic date—and the memory of four dead citizens was still painfully fresh. But the town was on a hair-trigger, around-the-clock watch because of an anonymous letter that had been sent to the town marshal.

The letter, which was reprinted in all the papers, said:

> Dear Sir:
>   I take the time to tell you and the city of Coffeyville that all the gang ain't dead yet, not by a hell of a sight, and don't you forget it. We shall have revenge for your killing of Bob and Grat and the rest. You people had no cause to take arms against the gang. The bankers will not help the widows of the men that got killed. Your time will soon come when you go into the grave and cash in your chips, so take warning.
>
>   Yours truly,
>   The Dalton Gang

The letter was postmarked from Arkansas City, and although the lawmen couldn't say for sure who wrote it, it shook folks up. There were rumors that a column of forty or fifty men was riding north to wipe out Coffeyville, and the railroad brought volunteers and guns from as far away as Kansas City to help protect the town.

There was, of course, no such army of outlaws. The Dalton Gang had never known more than a dozen members, and a good many of them had already been killed—shot to pieces in the streets of our hometown by people we'd grown up with. My brother Bob was leader of the gang and for bragging rights he wanted to rob two banks at once, which was one bank better than any job the James or Younger gangs had pulled. Even though we had already experienced our share of success and wet-your-pants terror in a dozen robberies from Oklahoma to California, Bob wanted one last big job to retire on.

But mostly, I think, Bob wanted to go down in the history books, and he got his wish. Not only did the raid buy the Dalton Gang a place next to the outfits headed by Jesse James and Cole Younger, it also put Coffeyville on the map. Overnight, because of the speed of the telegraph wires that fed the daily newspapers, everybody had heard of this sleepy little rail-and-cattle town that was like a hundred others except for one thing: the Dalton Gang.

The curious were flocking to Coffeyville almost before the smoke had cleared, to stick their fingers in one of the three hundred bullet holes in the Condon Bank and pay a nickel for a picture post-card of the four dead outlaws laid out like cord-wood in front of the city jail. If Bob could have known what an absolute casino the raid would prove to his old hometown, I think he would have chosen someplace else.

At the very least, I don't think he would have picked Coffeyville as the place to spend eternity in. I know I wouldn't have cared for it. But then, I was lucky.

Of the six Dalton Gang members who rode into Coffeyville the morning of the raid, four were dead, including my brothers Bob and Grat Dalton; a fifth member, my brother Emmett, was shot up so badly that they didn't know for a week or two if he would live; and the sixth man, who remained unidentified, escaped without a scratch.

There were some wild rumors circulating that the sixth rider was sometime gang member Bill Doolin or perhaps my brother Bob's girlfriend done up in men's clothing, but nobody had yet guessed the rider's real identity.

I know, because I was the sixth rider.

I had escaped the slaughter because my horse was tied away from the other horses, because there were so many people milling around with guns that one more wasn't noticed, and because for some reason I had a powerful load of luck on my side. After hiding out for a time in the Winding Stair Mountains of the Choctaw Nation—an area I had come to know during a stretch of hard luck when I was just a kid—I returned to Coffeyville to pay my respects at the graves of my brothers.

My stocking feet were aching from the cold as I picked my way carefully through the rows of tombstones toward potter's field, which lay at the eastern edge of the graveyard, hard against the Santa Fe tracks. It was there, I had been told, that my brothers Bob and Grat lay, their graves marked only by a bent iron pipe stuck into the ground.

I found the pipe by tripping over it.

"Well, Bob," I said to the ground as I got to my knees and brushed the dirt and gravel from my palms, "at least they made it easy to find you and Grat. How's it feel to lay forever under your last mistake?"

Even though I hated the idea that my brothers' graves were marked with a rusty piece of trash, I had to admit there was a sad fittingness to it. That section of pipe had been part of the hitching post in the alley where Bob left the horses, a block away from the banks and in a direct line of fire from the plaza. When things went wrong, that alley became a regular shooting gallery.

I sat down cross-legged on the grave and placed my right hand on the cold, moist earth. It sent a chill right up my bones to the elbow. It could have been the coolness of the night, or maybe it was the realization that, by rights, I should have been rotting down there with them.

"Boys, I don't know if you can hear me or not," I said, "but if you can, I'd rather you not let on. I've come here to say farewell, and perhaps a thing or two more. There's nothing I can say that will change things, of course, and it's all so much dust on the trail now. But I reckon that what I have to say will help me a sight more than it can ever help you."

I felt a little strange, talking to the ground, but I didn't know how else to do it. Regular folks get lots of opportunities to say good-bye, what with the deceased laid out all night in their best clothes in the parlor, and then of course later at the church or the cemetery, but outlaws hardly get a chance to tip their hats to the dead. I had considered writing a letter, but that was too risky because there were things I needed to say that the law would be right interested in. Besides, who would I get to deliver it?

I had truly wanted to attend the funeral, but considering how I had participated in the attempt to relieve the Condon Bank of its money, my attendance would not have been advisable. Bob and Grat, in fact, had been buried by strangers. Emmett was still too weak to move and the rest of the family was afraid to come to Coffeyville.

When they finally did come, led by my brother

Bill, they all signed a court paper that renounced any claim the family might have to the property left by Bob and Grat. That amounted to more than a thousand dollars' worth of guns, saddles, jewelry, and one surviving bay horse. Bob also had nine hundred dollars in cash from a previous holdup on him, and everything was disposed of by the court, with most of the items being bought at auction as souvenirs. I don't know what the court did with all that money, and maybe some of it went to help the widows and orphans of the raid, but it seems to me they could have spared some of it for a simple headstone.

"Bob, you should see the picture postcard they made of you," I said. "They stretched all four of you out like cordwood on a plank in front of the city jail so Tackett could take your picture. They put manacles on your wrists, as if you were still dangerous even though you were dead, and they laid a Winchester between you and Grat. I think it's your gun, Grat, but I can't be sure. And God knows why, but they drew in raggedy patches on your clothes and holes in your boots and socks. I reckon they don't like their desperadoes so well dressed, and tried to make you look like poor white trash. Your faces don't look natural, neither, because you're all gaunt and drawn and your lips are pulled back from your teeth. But I reckon you were dead a spell before they made the picture."

I reached inside my jacket and pulled out a twist of tobacco. I didn't chew, but my brothers enjoyed a plug now and then and I didn't think either of them cared especially for flowers. I placed the tobacco beneath the iron pipe.

"Bob, I shouldn't have let you talk us into this one, and I was a fool for letting you put Grat in charge of the Condon Bank job while you and Em took the First National.

"And, Grat, I should have gotten you out of the Condon Bank, even if I had to stick a gun in your ribs to do it. How could you believe that story about the vault being on a time lock and not opening for another fifteen minutes? All you had to do was walk over and try the damn door. Deciding to wait it out was like giving the folks on the plaza an engraved invitation to shoot the living hell out of us."

Grat was more than a mite thickheaded, and maybe he did the best he could, but Bob—who was blessed with approximately the share of brains that Grat was shorted—should have known better. You could count on Grat in a fight, with guns or knives or fists, but asking him to think was downright cruel.

"It's easy, I reckon, to look back and see where we went wrong," I said, "but it seemed damned hard at the time to stop, sort of like trying to keep water from running downhill. Both of you were so hell-bent on early graves that I'm surprised it didn't happen sooner. I'm just sorry that you took Powers and Broadwell and four innocent folks with you as well."

Wild Bill Powers was buried down there with my brothers because nobody had come forward to claim the outlaw's body. That may not be as awful as it sounds, because I don't think Powers was his real name, and there's no telling whether his kin knew where he lay. I never knew him that well in life, so I wasn't sure what to say to his corpse.

Dick Broadwell's folks came and dug him up and carted his remains back to Hutchinson a few days after he was buried in Elmwood Cemetery. They say that Broadwell was of good family, and I believe it, having seen the way he faced death there in the Condon Bank.

Of the four town folks that were killed, only one of them was a lawman. City Marshal Charlie Connelly, a former schoolteacher, had not even carried a gun to work with him that morning. Grat, already dying in the alley from a half-dozen wounds, killed Connelly while the marshal advanced on him with a borrowed gun.

The other three—merchant George Cubine, cobbler Charles Brown, and clerk Lucius Baldwin—were killed by Bob, who was a deadly shot with a Winchester.

"I hear that Em's going to keep his arm," I said, just as if Bob and Grat were still alive and we were sitting at the kitchen table exchanging news. "Old Doc Wells wanted to take it off," but Emmett wouldn't stand for it. Said he'd rather be dead than lose that arm. But I reckon he's getting better after all, because I read in the papers that they've moved him to the county jail at Independence."

The slug in his right arm was one of twenty-three wounds that Emmett received in the alley. Most of the damage was done by a double load of buckshot.

"It was one of the damnedest things I've ever seen," I said, and shook my head. "Our crazy brother Em—whom I never considered good for a damn thing except cooking, maybe—made it all the way to his horse with one of the moneybags. He could have gotten clean away. But instead he wheeled his horse around and plunged back into the alley. He reined his horse to a stop over you, Bob, and reached down his hand—but you were already dead, weren't you?"

Bob didn't answer.

In the dark silence I realized with terrible certainty that they were dead, dead beyond caring, dead as the dirt that held them. Even if the fairy tales the preachers told were true, they had assuredly gone to the bad place on the midnight express and were roasting for all the things they had done to folks.

"I'm mad as hell at both of you," I said, and despite myself tears began to roll down my cheeks. "You turn me into a common outlaw and then you get ourselves shot up, leaving me alone and Emmett facing a walk up the gallows. How're we supposed to stick together when half the gang is getting itself killed? How am I supposed to make a living when all the business experience I've had is robbing trains and banks? It doesn't look good to prospective employers, you know. And dammit, I miss both of you something fierce."

I wiped the tears away with the sleeve of my coat. To the north, the fire on the plaza was still blazing.

"I'm not going to follow you to an unmarked grave," I continued. "I've had enough of eating dust for breakfast and sleeping on the ground and being afraid to turn your back on people you meet. I'm not going to die with my boots on in the middle of the main street of some godforsaken cow town and wind up as a picture postcard with my hands cuffed and my face rigored back into a grin. I'm going to die peaceful, in a big feather bed, with my woman holding my hand and my grandkids in the next room—do you understand?"

I stopped, realizing that I was nearly shouting.

"But first," I said, "I need to figure out how to bust Emmett out of jail."

Two

Even with a Winchester in one hand it was pie to jump up on the locomotive tender as the *Express* slowed down to approach the station at Caney. I knew Bill Doolin was right behind me because I could hear his boots on the iron rungs. It was still bitterly cold, but I scarcely noticed it; perhaps it had something to do with risking death yet again, but I felt incredibly alive climbing onto a train with a gun in my hand.

It was something like buck fever, only worse. Better, maybe.

We scrambled over the top of the tender and pointed our rifles at the engineer and his stoker. Doolin was breathing a mite heavily from the exertion, but I reckoned it was normal for a man of his age—he was thirty-four, exactly twice as old as me—and he had to pause a moment before he spoke.

"I'd be obliged," he finally said in his Arkansas drawl, "if you gentlemen would pull this train right on past the station." His voice was muffled by the blue kerchief tied around the lower part of his face, and he gestured down the track with a twitch of the rifle barrel for emphasis.

"You're holding the gun," the white-haired engineer said.

The old man spat tobacco juice out the window and with a gloved hand ratcheted the throttle back a couple of stops. The locomotive huffed deeply and we drew away from the yellow light thrown by the depot windows. Inside, the station agent was trussed and gagged behind his desk, and his brass telegraph key was useless because the lines had been roped and dragged down.

It had been Doolin's idea to send a revenge letter to Coffeyville and then hit the Missouri Pacific at Caney, eighteen miles to the west, instead. While every lawman in a fifty-mile radius was standing guard on the plaza, protecting Coffeyville from a hoax, we were busy robbing the *Express*. It was a plan that would have aroused the deepest jealousy in my brother Bob.

Although I had sworn off a life of crime after the Coffeyville raid, I soon found that getting quit of the outlaw business wasn't that simple. I had sought out Doolin for help in saving Emmett from the hangman's rope, and Doolin had pointed out that a jailbreak wasn't something that just one or two men could accomplish. What you needed was a gang to do it right, he said, so why didn't I join up with the new outfit he was starting?

I agreed because my greater obligation, it seemed, was to place Emmett's skin ahead of my own tarnished if immortal soul. I am also ashamed to report that I was always partial to the concept of train robbery, which is generally conducted well away from the vicinity of hardware stores and amateur marksmen.

Boiler sparks swirled from the stack as the train

moved through the darkness. We sat on the top of the tender, our rifles trained on the cab. The engineer seemed to be taking things calmly enough, but the stoker—a big, broad-chested fellow with coal-black hair—was shaking like a leaf.

"Right about here would be fine," Doolin commanded when we were a half mile from the station. The engineer engaged the brake and the train began to slow. We slipped down into the cab and Doolin told the stoker to go back and uncouple the combination express-and-baggage car, which was immediately behind the tender, from the rest of the train. The big fellow looked at us with eyes the size of saucers but did not move.

"Paolo don't speak English," the engineer said, and spat tobacco juice out the side of the train. "All he understands is Portuguese, and unless one of you gents speak the lingo, you're not going to get much out of him."

"Then tell him to unhook the express car," Doolin said.

"Hell, I don't speak it," the engineer said. "I tell him 'dammit' to stoke the boiler and 'sumbitch' to stop, and he gets the drift. We haven't moved on to the finer points of conversation yet."

"Wonderful," Doolin said. "What's your name, Pop?"

"Eggleston."

"Okay, Eggleston, go unhook the express car yourself, and do it pronto. Go with him, Kid, and ventilate him if he tries anything clever."

"You don't have to worry about me," the engineer said as he climbed down from the cab to the roadbed, "I ain't stupid enough to try anything brave. But there's going to be a freight coming down the line in about twenty minutes, and if you don't let us get those cars onto a siding, or at least send a man with a lantern back down the tracks, there's going to be a helluva crash."

Doolin paused, unsure of what to do.

"I think you're lying," Doolin said at last. "There ain't no freight comes through here after the *Express*."

"Suit yourself," the engineer said. "But you're killing innocent people."

"Where's the nearest switch?" Doolin asked.

"Back at the station," Eggleston said.

Doolin cursed.

"Even if he is lying," I said, "it won't hurt to send the conductor back down the tracks swinging a lantern. It'll take at least half an hour for them to make it back to the depot, and by the time the word gets out about the robbery, we'll be long gone."

Doolin nodded.

I walked behind Eggleston to the rear of the express car. As he did the uncoupling the lights inside the express car went out, and we could hear the messenger barricading the door with furniture. I crouched down behind the corner of the car, expecting bullets to start whizzing at any minute, but none came.

"Roust your conductor and tell him to take off down the tracks with a lantern," I said, "and do it double quick."

Eggleston climbed up the platform of the coach car and called out until the conductor, a small man with a dirty uniform, inquired sleepily what was the matter.

"We're being robbed," Eggleston said. "Take your lantern and hotfoot it back toward the station so as to warn the freight crew that the cars are stalled on the tracks."

The man nodded and started to dodge back into the coach.

"Hold it," I said, raising the rifle. "You stand right here on the platform where I can see you until we pull away. Then you can fetch your lantern. Understand?"

He nodded.

"Good. Come on, Eggleston."

I slid close along the side of the express car, to make it hard for somebody inside to get a bead on me, and breathed easier when Eggleston and I reached the locomotive again. I followed the engineer up into the cab.

"Let's move out," Doolin said.

"Dammit," Eggleston barked.

"Dammit," Paulo repeated. Seemingly relieved to have something to do, Paulo unlatched the fire door with his shovel and began scooping coal into the furnace. As we pulled away from the coaches I stuck my head out the side window and could see a red lantern bobbing off down the tracks.

"The messenger bolted the doors and barricaded himself inside, like we reckoned he would," I told Doolin, then asked: "What's the time?" Doolin took the pocket watch from his vest and held the face toward the open firebox. "It's twenty minutes after ten," he said.

It had been only five minutes since we boarded the train, although it seemed like longer. If I had learned anything from the Coffeyville raid, it was that time was against you; the longer you stayed on a job, the more likely it was that you'd get killed. Doolin and I had an agreement that if the robbery took more than fifteen minutes, we would give it up, even if it meant leaving empty-handed.

We had Eggleston stop the train in a deep cut a mile farther down the track. Oliver Yantis and Bitter Creek Newcomb were waiting there for us, along with the horses.

Bitter Creek was a member of the old gang and we had ridden many a mile together, and I had often put up with his singing about how he was a lone wolf from Bitter Creek and it was his night to howl. Yantis had never pulled a job with us, but he had often brought us grub or given us a place to hide. Also, Bitter Creek was sweet on Ol's sister, even though she was married—but that never seemed to matter much to most of the boys.

"Okay, shut her down," Doolin said.

"Sumbitch," Eggleston ordered.

"Sumbitch," Paolo replied, and closed the firebox.

"I'd like you gentlemen to climb down so we can keep an eye on you," Doolin said. Eggleston left the cab easily enough, but Paolo had to be convinced by a lot of motioning with our guns, and even then he wanted to take his shovel. We insisted he leave it behind.

"What's the messenger's name?" Doolin asked.

"Maxwell," Eggleston replied.

"Is he alone in there?"

"As far as I know."

Doolin inched around the corner of the tender.

"Maxwell, you might as well give it up," he shouted. "There are plenty of us and only one of you. Why get yourself killed protecting somebody else's money? The smart thing to do would be to swing open that door and let us in."

Gunfire blossomed from one of the express car's forward windows and a bullet ricocheted off the tender close to Doolin's head. Doolin ducked—a meaningless but automatic reflex—thumbed back the hammer of his Winchester, and sent a round right back.

"Aim high," Doolin instructed. "We may need him to—"

Doolin's words were lost in a thunder of revolver blasts. The rest of us scurried to find cover
behind rocks and trees alongside the tracks and we
emptied our rifles into the top half of the car, although Yantis seemed to be shooting a bit low. The
night was bright with muzzle flashes and punctuated
by the roar of gunfire and the tinkle of spent cartridges as they rained down. When we had finished,
the express car was riddled with bullet holes and
gun smoke lay thick over the roadbed.

"Have you had enough?" Doolin called as he
thumbed shells into the magazine of his Winchester.

"I'm hit," Maxwell called back. "I think my
arm is broken."

"That's what you get for trying to kill me,"
Doolin said. "Open up!"

"Go to hell."

"What time is it?" I asked.

"Twenty-five after," Doolin said, consulting his
watch. "Boys, did you bring the persuader?"

"Yep," Bitter Creek said, and held up a canvas
bag. "Is it time to use it?"

"It's time," Doolin said. "It was nice knowing
you, Maxwell. You put up a good scrap, but we've
had enough of your foolishness. Stand back, everybody, because we're going to blow this express car
clean into the next county."

"Dynamite?" Maxwell called. "You're going to
use dynamite?"

"Go ahead, boys," Doolin said. "He had his
chance."

Bitter Creek took a bundle of dynamite and
pushed a long fuse into one end. He struck a match
on his belt and lit a cheroot, then held the dynamite
in one hand and puffed on the cigar with the other.

"Where do you want it, boss?" he asked.

"Just toss it up underneath the door," Doolin said. "How many sticks you have tied together?"

"Five."

"Reckon that ought to do it."

Bitter Creek took one last drag on the cigar and held the glowing end to the fuse. It ignited with a sputter. He let the fuse uncoil to the ground, then took the bundle of dynamite in his right hand and prepared to toss it.

"Wait!" the messenger shouted, and threw his revolver out. "I surrender. I'm opening up." There were sounds of furniture being dragged away and then the clatter of the bolt as it was being thrown back. Suddenly the door rolled open and there was Maxwell, with his hands up and blood dripping from his left arm.

"Put it out," Doolin called.

"Shoot," Bitter Creek grumbled, but pulled the burning, half-consumed fuse out of the dynamite and threw it on the ground. "I was just about ready to toss it." He returned the bundle to the canvas bag.

"It wasn't real, was it?" Maxwell asked sheepishly.

"Yes, it was," Doolin replied as he climbed up into the express car. "I don't believe in bluffs. We would have blown the door clean off if you hadn't been fortunate enough to see the error of your ways. Now turn up the lights in here and open that safe."

The bullet that pierced Maxwell's upper arm did not strike bone and Doolin pronounced that he would live. One-handed, the messenger spun the combination to the through safe and swung open the door, and while Yantis and Bitter Creek held their guns on the train crew, Doolin and I scooped the money out into a grain sack I'd brought.

The take was disappointing. We counted less
than fifty dollars in paper money and a few odd dollars in silver as we took the money out of the safe.
On the messenger's desk was a recent edition of the
Caney Chronicle, and I noticed DALTONS over an
item on the front page, so I stuffed the newspaper
into my pocket.

"Damn," Doolin said. "That's it?"

"That's it," Maxwell replied.

"It can't be," I said. "Nobody risks getting
killed to protect a lousy fifty dollars. He's hidden it
somewhere."

Doolin and I glanced around the interior of the
car. There were dozens of pigeonholes and nooks
and crannies where he could have hidden the money,
but I didn't think any of them were big enough to
hold much. Besides, we didn't have time to check
them all. Then I put my hand on the stove. It was
cold, and the floor was still wet from where he had
doused the fire with water carried from the iron
drinking-water tank.

"The crafty bastard has hidden it in the stove,"
I said.

I swung open the door to the firebox and there,
hidden amongst the ashes, were several bundles of
new money.

Most of the loot was in notes issued by the First
National Bank of Kansas City and was intended as
payroll for way stations down the line. We didn't
stop to count it as we raked it into the sack, but
later we divided a little more than a thousand dollars of the banknotes and some worn greenbacks, all
of which would spend nicely.

The railroad would tell the newspapers the next
day that we got less than one hundred dollars, of
course, but that was just Hoyle for them: they'd as

soon kiss their grandmothers than admit that crime not only paid, but paid right well.

"Time?" I asked, when we had cleaned out the safe.

"Ten thirty-one," Doolin answered.

"We're a minute behind schedule. Let's clear out," I said.

"Get down, all of you," Doolin barked. "If you so much as raise your heads up, I'll blow them off, and you keep them down until we're well gone."

Eggleston pulled Paolo down onto the roadbed with him while Maxwell stretched out on the floor of the express car. Doolin relieved the messenger of his watch and told him it was the least he could contribute after all the trouble he'd been.

Yantis, meanwhile, had led our horses up to the door of the car. I jumped onto Cimarron and tied the grain sack to the saddle horn so I wouldn't lose it if we were forced to ride hard. But that didn't appear likely. The track was dark and quiet in both directions.

Doolin mounted, then tossed me the stolen pocket watch.

"Keep it," he said. "You'll need it for the next job."

Three

We divided the loot from the train robbery and each struck out on his own, planning to rendezvous in a few days at Ingalls in Oklahoma Territory. Because of its location in the former Unassigned Lands, far from the railroads and major trails, Ingalls had become notorious as an outlaw hideout.

After two days of easy riding, without having seen so much as a mail hack, Cimarron threw a shoe not long after we crossed the Arkansas River. I ended up walking him across a good deal of the Pawnee Reserve for fear that he would go lame in the leg or shoulder.

Cimarron and I reached Ingalls late in the afternoon. My clothes were soaked with sweat and I was so covered with gritty red dust that I could taste it every time I swallowed. I was not used to walking and my feet were paining me something awful. My throat was raw and I had drunk my fill of the tepid water from the canteen. What I wanted was something cold to drink and a place in the shade where I could put my feet up, maybe even a bath. But your horse always comes first.

At the corner of First and Ash, where the wagon road entered town, there was a blacksmith shop run by an Army of the Potomac veteran named Alonzo Light. I led Cimarron to the open double door of the shop and dropped his reins there, knowing he would stay put until I came to get him.

I found Light at the forge, working a wheel rim. Sparks showered from the hoop with each blow of the hammer, and the sound was deafening. A kid of thirteen or fourteen, maybe an apprentice, was pumping the bellows. Light was bald, but made up for the lack of hair on his scalp with a graying beard that reached his chest. His arms were bare and they were roped with muscle from years of smithing. He was tall—more than six feet, I judged—and had a long, thin nose upon which were perched a pair of eyeglasses. His height, combined with his horse face and the spectacles, created the impression that he was perpetually looking down upon the world.

I stood watching him work for some time, anxious to be on my way toward a cool drink and a bath, but not wanting to interrupt. It wasn't that he had me dogged in any way—I knew that no amount of muscle and bone could stand up to what I carried on my hip—but I was fascinated by the concentration Light displayed, and how regular his rhythm was as he methodically worked the rim back into shape. I have always been taken by folks who could create things, who could make something useful or beautiful or, if they're lucky, both. I had not learned much that was practical in the years I had been riding with my brothers, nothing but rustling and robbing and running from the law. Drinking and whoring when you had a moment to catch your breath, never sitting with your back to the door, always sleeping with one eye open. Killing and dying when they finally run you to earth. The dying was easy. It was the living that was hard.

It occurred to me at that moment, watching Alonzo Light absorbed in concentration as he contributed something useful to the world, that I had never learned how to make a living—no, that was not quite right. It was that I had *never learned how to live*. The thought rang through me like one of the blows from the blacksmith's hammer. I felt sick inside, like there was a hole in me the wind could blow through.

Light finished with the rim and plunged it, with a hiss and a wisp of steam, into a vat of water. He carefully laid aside the hammer and wiped his hands on his leather apron.

"Your horse," he said. "Must have thrown a shoe." Without waiting for any comment from me, he walked over toward Cimarron. The horse let him approach to within six feet, then backed away, dragging the reins. I walked over and gently grasped a cheek strap, and in low tones spoke to Cimarron. Light knelt and lifted the hoof, inspecting the frog and the nails left in the wall. Then he released the hoof and ran his hand slowly up Cimarron's leg to his shoulder.

Light stood.

"This is a fine horse," he said. "He doesn't appear to be the worse for wear."

"I walked him in."

"Oh?" Light said. "From where?"

"About ten miles this side of the Arkansas River."

"That's a far piece to walk an animal."

"This horse means a lot to me."

"That's obvious," he said. Then he looked

down his long nose at me and asked, "What were you doing up that way?"

I took a moment too long to answer, and from the glint in his eyes I believed he knew I was about to lie. But since I had taken the trouble to think of something, I let it rip: I was a stock buyer from Arkansas.

Light snorted.

"This town has about all the cattle buyers it can handle," he said. "You'll find your colleagues down at the Ransom and Murray Saloon, or perhaps over at Sadie Comley's whorehouse."

I should have been a little more original—every outlaw since the days of the James and Younger gangs had always said they were out-of-state stock buyers, to explain their guns, their hard-ridden horses, and their large amounts of cash.

"Damn, but if you haven't caught me in a bold-faced lie," I said. "I don't know who you think my friends are, but the truth of the matter—"

"Son, you had best stop," Light said. "I'm too old to listen to any more foolishness. I'll shoe your animal for you, and I'll do a damn good job, because I'm the best there is, at least in this Territory. But don't take me for a fool. I don't want to know where the money you're going to pay me with came from."

Then he turned away.

While Light fetched his farrier's wooden box of tools, I uncinched Cimarron's saddle and removed it, along with the blanket, the Winchester in its scabbard, my bedroll, and the saddlebags. The bit and bridle would remain until Cimarron had been reshod. By now, the kid who had been working the bellows had come to look Cimarron over. He took an apple out of the pocket of his coveralls and started to hold it out, then thought it best to ask my permission.

"Go ahead," I said. "Cimarron will like it."

He held the apple in the flat of his palm while Cimarron gobbled it up. The kid had red hair and blue eyes and so many freckles across the bridge of his nose that it looked like some kind of mask. His shoulders, which were bare beneath his worn coveralls, were also freckled. He smiled broadly as the horse finished the apple. I liked this kid, who seemed to have a natural enthusiasm for life.

"What's your name?" I asked.

"Del Simmons, sir."

"You seem to get along with Cimarron right well," I said. "After he's shod, I'll give you four bits—in advance—if you'll take him over to Ransom's livery, brush him down, and see that he gets squared away proper. Del, do you think you can do that?"

"Yes, sir," he answered. "I'll haul your tack over to the livery, too."

Light came back with his tools and set to work dressing Cimarron's foot while Del held him still. "I'll have to take off the other shoe to make him the same height," he said.

I nodded, picked up the Winchester, and slung the saddlebags, which contained my share of the Caney train robbery, over my left shoulder. I fished fifty cents from my jeans pocket and gave it to Del, then asked Light how much I owed him.

"We'll settle up tomorrow," he said, without looking up.

I shrugged and gave Del a wave as I set off south down Ash Street. In the next block there was a restaurant and a dry-goods store, and where Second crossed there was a public well in the middle of the street. I stopped at the well, soaked my kerchief in the water, and wiped the trail dust from my hands and face.

On the southwest corner of the intersection was a small unpainted building with a false front and a weather-beaten sign that said simply SALOON. It was pretty much as I remembered it, except someone had tacked a Pabst beer sign onto one corner of the structure. Inside, there was only one room, but it did have a full-length bar and a number of green felt poker tables. I noted that the mirror behind the bar had been replaced.

I stopped just inside the door, carrying the Winchester at my side, my hand in the trigger guard and my finger on the hammer. It was dark inside, because the shades were pulled down over the two windows in the front of the building, and I was relieved when I heard a familiar voice call out.

It was Bill Doolin.

"Come on over," he said in his Arkansas drawl. There were ten or twelve people in the place—which meant it was downright full, that's how small it was—and Doolin and Bitter Creek Newcomb were sitting at the farthest table from the door with their backs to the wall. Doolin was drinking beer. Bitter Creek, who was drinking whiskey, had his feet up on the table. "I expected you here a mite sooner," Doolin said. "You didn't have any shooting trouble, did you?"

"Nothing like that," I said, leaning the Winchester against the wall and dropping the saddle wallets over the back of the chair next to Doolin. "My horse threw a shoe."

When I sat down Bitter Creek put his feet back on the floor. He apparently had already had several drinks—his eyes were blurry and his speech was beginning to slur. Every once in a while he would throw his head back and howl like a wolf.

"How about you—any problems?" I asked
Doolin.

"Nary a one."

"What's wrong with Bitter Creek?" I asked.

"Oh, he's got himself worked into a froth over
a girl he's been courting," Doolin said. "Her name's
Rose Dunn and her big brother doesn't like the idea
of her sparking with an outlaw. Says it ain't becoming."

"Hell," Bitter Creek said. "Me and Bee Dunn
used to ride together—I still consider him my friend.
And here he says I'm not good enough to court his
sister. Well, to hell with him."

Doolin drained his beer, then motioned to the
bartender. Two cold bottles of beer and another
whiskey were brought to the table and Doolin paid
for all of it. Normally I don't drink, but I was hot
and I didn't want to offend Doolin by refusing. It
tasted better than I had ever remembered beer tast-
ing.

The bartender, a man named Murray, hesitated
a moment at the table. From the corner of my eye I
saw him staring at me, as if he were trying to work
up the courage to say something.

"Is there something I can do for you?" I asked
into my beer.

"No," he said. "Well, perhaps. I mean, you are
the Choctaw Kid, aren't you?"

The room suddenly got very quiet.

"Look here," Doolin told the bartender, "it
ain't any of your business who he might be. Besides,
you know that out here, folks don't ask names."

"What I meant was that I've seen the Kid before," the bartender said. "He was here in the saloon a few months back—he killed Bloody Bill
Towerly at that table right over there. I saw it hap-

pen, it was just like lightning, three shots that damn near went into the same hole in Towerly's chest."

"The group wasn't that good," I said.

William Towerly was the bastard who killed my brother Frank in the Arkansas River Bottoms a few years back, and I was not ashamed to admit that I had shot him to death not so long ago in that very saloon—although I had let him pull on me first.

"What's your point, mister?" I asked.

"Well," he stammered, "I just wanted to ask if you wouldn't mind going outside if you have any of the same kind of trouble. It took us a helluva long time to get that mirror replaced—I know you paid for it, but it had to come all the way from St. Louis—and I'd hate to see it shot up again."

"I'll do my best," I allowed.

Murray nodded and went back behind his bar. Doolin tried to suppress a smile.

"You mirror-killing bastard," Bitter Creek said.

"I heard about Towerly," Doolin said between sips of beer. "He needed killing. But it's a shame about the mirror. It kind of makes me sick inside just thinking about it."

I knew it would be a spell before they quit chewing on that particular rag, so I just sat there, drank my beer, and took it. When there was a pause in their fun, I took out the newspaper I had picked up in the express car.

"There's news of Emmett here," I said.

"From the sound of your voice, it's not good," Doolin said. "Read it to me."

After two days of reading it, I had committed the item to memory. "It's dated Coffeyville, October tenth," I said, "and it says that if there is any change in the condition of Emmett Dalton, it is for the worse, and that all visitors are now denied admittance. They don't expect him to live."

Doolin nodded sadly.

"There's also an item here about the funeral of Lucius Baldwin at Burlington, his hometown." My brother Bob had killed Baldwin in the alley behind the First National Bank in Coffeyville. "They say it was one of the largest funerals ever seen there. There's another story from the banks denying rumors that they recovered more money from the bodies of the Dalton brothers than was lost in the raid."

"Did they?" Doolin asked.

"I don't know," I said. "But I know that Bob had nine hundred dollars in his pocket when he rode into town. I'll bet it didn't go through probate."

When I had finished the bottle I stood and gathered my things. I wanted someplace to wash the trail dust off. I was also feeling melancholy about Emmett and didn't want company.

"Thanks for the beer," I said.

"You looked like you needed it," Doolin said.

"Where can I find a room and a bath?" I asked.

"Well, you can sleep at the O.K. Hotel, which is east on Second Street. It's not really much of a hotel, but it's the only one in town—there's a few bunks in the attic that cowboys use because they're cheap. If you'd like something a little friendlier, with a good bath, you can go to Sadie Comley's place. It's down the same street, you can't miss it."

I nodded and turned toward the door. The heft of the Winchester and the weight of the saddlebags on my left shoulder, with the two hundred and fifty dollars in loot they contained, was reassuring. Behind me, Bitter Creek howled again and ordered another whiskey. It looked like he was working himself into a real high lonesome.

• • •

Sadie Comley's place was a whorehouse, but all I wanted was a bath. I walked through the front door with my gear and stood for a moment, taking in the gaming tables and a couple of girls who were sitting around in their underwear. It must have been a slow time of day, because they didn't seem to have any business. It was a small house—there were only four rooms, including the parlor, and no upstairs—but it was right respectable for being in the middle of nowhere in Oklahoma Territory.

A big woman who I reckoned for the madam—mainly because she was dressed—looked at me standing in the doorway, with my Winchester at my side.

"Honey," she said, "you can put that down—the only gun you'll need here is the one in your pants."

The girls laughed.

They were both young, about my age or a little older. One was a dark-haired girl with brown eyes who seemed sort of timid, and she was straight as a rail. The other had blue eyes and blond hair with reddish highlights, and she covered her mouth as she laughed. The blonde made up for what the other girl lacked, and I found myself staring.

"Sorry," I said at last.

"Come on in," the madam said, "and shut the door behind you. My name is Sadie and you're welcome here as long as you have money and act like a gentleman. The girls are Hannah and Lucinda. You're welcome to relax and get to know them a little, first. Would you like a drink?"

"No, ma'am," I said. "What I would really like to start with is a bath."

"That's an excellent idea, young man," Sadie said. "I believe we can accommodate you directly. Hannah, would you check the stove and see that the water gets heated? Make sure there is plenty of it. Lucinda, why don't you show him to the back room and get the tub ready? Now, let's see. That'll be fifty cents for the bath . . . unless, of course, you'd like your back or some other part of your anatomy scrubbed."

Lucinda, for that was the name of the fair-haired girl, smiled and took me by the arm. I was tired and dirty, and had really only wanted a bath, but I hadn't counted on meeting anybody like Lucinda. It wasn't just that she was beautiful, but it was the way she moved and the way she *smelled*— clean and alive, like a flower garden after a spring rain. I reached into the saddlebag, pulled out a ten-dollar note, and handed it to Sadie. There are some kinds of loneliness, I had discovered, that only a woman can ease.

Four

Lucky Lucinda led me to the back room, where the tub—really a large wooden washtub—was hidden behind a blanket draped over a rope. I unstrapped my gun belt. She took the rig from me and held it for a moment, fingering the beadwork on the holster and touching the walnut grips of the Colts.

"Have you ever killed anybody?" she asked.

"Yes," I said.

She started to lay the rig on the bed, but I asked her to keep it close by, so she hung it by a peg on the wall above the tub.

"Your boots," Lucinda said. "Let's get them off."

I sat in a chair while she straddled my right leg and pulled. My feet were swollen and the boot did not want to come off. When it finally did, it felt like it was taking the hide with it. The other did not come any easier. With my boots off, I could see that the soles of both feet were covered with blisters and a fair amount of crusted blood.

31

"Damn, mister," Lucinda said. "Your dogs are a mess."

"They'll heal," I said. "Look here, has anyone told you how absolutely *good* you smell? I mean, it's not like perfume or anything—it's better."

"A couple of cowboys have mentioned it," she said. "But I didn't know what they were talking about. But you're right, it's not lilac water or powder, it's just me."

She sat on my lap and started undoing my shirt. She felt like she weighed hardly anything at all, as if she were made of feathers or maybe clouds. I reached up and stroked her hair. It was an awkward movement, because I felt coarse compared to her, and my hand seemed like a stump. But she smiled. When her lips parted I saw that she was missing most of the right dogtooth in her upper row of teeth.

It was like biting into the reddest, ripest apple you've ever seen and finding a worm. But then, it wasn't like that at all, because the apple doesn't care how you feel about it.

Lucinda put a hand to her mouth and turned away. Tears came to her eyes. "I'm sorry," she mumbled. "Mrs. Comley has told me to be careful of keeping my mouth shut. Except for, well, you know."

I didn't know.

"You have nothing to be sorry for," I said lamely. "I don't mind, truly I don't." Then I lied: "You're still every bit as beautiful as when I first saw you."

She still wouldn't look at me.

I felt rotten. If only I hadn't started so.

"I think I understand why the cowboys named you Lucky," I said. "I feel lucky just to be near you.

Compared to how beautiful you are, I feel like some ugly cowhand."

"Oh, but you're not," she said, and slowly let her hand drop from her mouth. "You're so different than the others. You're handsome—well, Bitter Creek is handsome, too—but you're handsome in a better way. You aren't vain like Bitter Creek. I wanted you to pick me the moment I saw you standing in the doorway with your saddlebags and your guns."

"You did?"

She nodded.

"And I know you ain't no cowboy. Why, just look at your hands. The only calluses you have are from handling a six-shooter. You're an outlaw. That excites me."

I didn't say anything.

Hannah came in and dumped another couple of buckets into the tub. Lucinda waited until she was gone before continuing.

"Thank you for telling me you don't mind about my teeth," she said as she finished stripping off my shirt. "Although I think you're just being kind—I've studied myself in the looking glass. Now, stand up and let's get those pants off."

"You're still beautiful, no matter what you think of yourself," I said. "Turn around, please."

"Why?" she asked with a laugh.

"Because I promised to act like a gentleman."

She turned her back while I slipped out of the rest of my clothes. I was in an embarrassing condition, you might say, so I quickly eased myself into the tub. The water felt blessed.

"Okay," I said.

She knelt beside the tub.

"What do you want?" she asked.

I handed her the bar of soap.

She scrubbed my back. It felt wonderful, and I sighed with pleasure. She leaned down and kissed my ear.

"What do you want me to call you?" she asked.

"Whatever you want."

"No, be serious. What do Doolin and the boys call you?"

"Kid," I said.

"Don't you have a first name?"

"Sam."

"Good," she said.

I closed my eyes and rested my head on the back of the tub. It had been a long spell since I had gotten to relax—since before the Coffeyville raid, in fact. It was true what they said about no rest for the wicked. But then rest was so delicious when it finally came that it almost made up for it.

"Sam," Lucinda said. "The reason the cowboys call me Lucky—it's not what you think."

"Tell me about it," I said sleepily.

"No. I don't want to discuss about it. It makes me sad."

"Then tell me about yourself."

"Why?" she asked, then laughed. She was rubbing my shoulders now. "Nobody's ever asked me to talk before frigging. At least, not just talk, without talking dirty."

"I want to know more about you," I said. "Where you grew up. What your family was like, and how—"

"How I came to be a whore," she said.

"Well, I did wonder," I said. "You being so young and beautiful and all. It must be an awfully tragic tale."

"Not so tragic as stupid," she said, and squeezed out the sponge over my back. "I grew up in an orphanage in Kansas City, and when I was twelve I was adopted by an old couple from Atchison that wanted a servant instead of a daughter—actually the old goat insisted on quite a bit more than that. So I put up with it for a while, but ran away with a drummer when I was fifteen, but the thing was that he had a wife and three kids back home in Springfield. I spent some time on my own, nearly starved to death, then hooked up with a gambling feller named Darlington who beat me when he was drunk. He's the one what brought me here to Ingalls. The bastard lost me in a card game right in that front parlor. I couldn't stomach the new man, so after he got his money's worth I asked Mrs. Comley to take me in. I guessed I might as well be selling what I had been giving away right along."

"How old are you now?"

"Don't really know," she said. "It depends on when my birthday is, and nobody knows that. They reckoned at the orphanage that it must have been in the late fall, because I wasn't very old when I was brought in. So I must be nearly seventeen now."

"Why didn't you just pick a day and make it your birthday?"

"It wouldn't feel right," she said. "I'd have to *know*."

I was just a little older than she was, but I didn't tell her so. She seemed to think I was quite a bit older, and that's the way it felt best.

Her hands left my back and I heard the rustle of clothing. Suddenly she was in the tub with me, pink and beautiful and proud of it, and the water was sloshing out onto the floor. There was just enough for both of us in the tub, and our legs overlapped. I

had never taken a bath with a girl before. I wasn't
sleepy any longer.

She leaned forward, took my face in her hands,
and kissed me.

I sighed another one of those sighs like I had
died and gone to heaven.

"Outlaw," she said, "if you think this is good,
just stick around—you bought me for all night."

Five

Doolin and the others were waiting for me the next morning at the Rock Fort, which was a glorified cave located near the Cimarron River on the Dunn homestead, a few miles southeast of Ingalls. The "fort" was not much more than a wall of stones piled across the entrance to the cave. Although the boys had made a regular little house inside, complete with bunks and a fireplace, I never felt safe there. Perhaps it was the peculiar way the oldest of the four brothers, Bee Dunn, seemed to size up guests—as if he were always reckoning who would be the first to clear leather or how much wood he'd need to make a coffin. Whatever the reason, I was glad my money was hidden and thankful when Doolin announced the gang would be heading out soon for another job.

Doolin kept us in suspense for a few days while he considered our options. Mostly he and Bitter Creek drank, or played cards, or target-practiced. I read. Wherever cowboys have made a place home for more than a day or two, whether it is a bunkhouse or line shack or jail cell, you can usually find something left by the previous occupants to read. The Rock Fort library consisted of a couple of romances by Walter Scott, a seed catalog, and a book of stories by Washington Irving. Bitter Creek, however, had the attentions of Rose Dunn to keep him occupied.

Rose was not the most beautiful girl I had ever seen—her nose was a little too big for the rest of her face—but she had a quality that made men ready to kill each other for, even if she was only fourteen years old. It wasn't just animal magnetism, but something else; her soul seemed to shine in her face when she laughed, and if her gaze were directed at you, a little of that good feeling would rub off. It was in the way she moved, too, and in her dark hair and eyes, some kind of smoldering spark always wanting to burst into flame. That flame burned for Bitter Creek, who hands down was the finest specimen in the Wild Bunch—tall, with clear blue eyes and dark hair and mustache, and a reckless, confident way.

Rose lived with her mother and stepfather, Doc Call, in Ingalls, but was a frequent visitor to the Rock Fort. The way she and Bitter Creek enjoyed each other just made me feel worse about Lucinda. Bee Dunn hung around a lot as well, asking lots of questions about the gang, trying to appear like he was everybody's friend and glowering at Bitter Creek when he thought nobody was looking.

I was flopped down on a bunk in the Rock Fort reading *Ivanhoe* for the third time when Doolin finally allowed that the next job would be a bank. Bitter Creek perked up his ears and took a seat near the fire to hear what Doolin had to say. I laid the book aside and sat up.

"A bank?" I asked. "I thought we might do another train."

Doolin shook his head.

"You need fewer men to hit a bank than a train," he said. "Three or four will do. And with trains you've got to know in advance how much money they're carrying, or the job might not be worth doing. But with a bank, you are reasonably sure there's going to be a considerable amount of loot—especially if you hit a bank where the pickings are rich, like in the cattle country around Dodge."

Bitter Creek nodded.

I didn't like it. The last bank job I had been on put two of my brothers in the ground and all but killed the third. Banks were not good for Daltons. They tended to be too close to hardware stores, and hardware stores had plenty of guns. My brother Bob should have learned that lesson, but he didn't—and paid with his life, and that of Grat, too. But I couldn't just come out and say I was against the plan. They would have thought I was yellow. So I took a different tack.

"What bank were you planning to hit?" I asked as casual as I could.

"I don't have no favorites," Doolin said. "My mind is to take an easy ride up the Cimarron River and do some scouting into Kansas. Study up some on the towns and banks. Get the lay of the land straight in our minds."

"I wouldn't want to hit anything in Dodge," Bitter Creek said, smoothing his mustache with his thumb. "That Chalk Beeson has more sand than most county sheriffs. I wouldn't want him leading a posse after me."

"Well," Doolin said easy, "there are plenty of banks in the little towns around Dodge City. We can find one a few miles away from Dodge City, so by the time Beeson hears about us, we'll be damn near

home. Being strictly a county sheriff, he can't follow
us once we skip back into the Territory."

Bitter Creek nodded.

"Kid," Doolin said. "Shall we go a-calling?"

Doolin was making it sound too easy. There
were a thousand things that could go wrong with a
bank job, all of them deadly, and hardware stores
were at the top of the list. I didn't mind taking a
risk—hell, all of life is a risk, even if you lock yourself in a room with indoor plumbing and have
your meals brought in—but I would rather take
a carefully calculated risk where banks were con-
cerned.

"Count me in," I said, "but only if we all agree
on the bank we hit. If one of us says nay, then the
job is off. That's the democratic way to do it."

Bitter Creek looked puzzled.

"I didn't think we were runnin' the Wild Bunch
by committee," he said. "Bill here is the leader of the
gang. Why, I think he did a fine job on the express."

"I'm not saying he didn't. I just have a little
more experience with banks than either of you, and
I want to feel comfortable with things before we
move in."

Doolin smiled.

"Kid," he said, "I never knew you to be so
spooked over a job before. You can pull out if you
want, and Bitter Creek and I will wish you well. But
tell me one thing—what're you afraid of?"

"Hardware stores," I said. "I just don't want
any hardware stores near the bank."

Doolin chewed it over for a spell, then nodded.

"It's something I should have thought of," he
said. "It happened at Northfield and again at
Coffeyville. We don't need to make the list any
longer. Bitter Creek?"

"No hardware stores," he said.

• • •

So it was in the middle of October when we started out from the Dunn Ranch and followed the Cimarron River northwest on a scouting expedition into Kansas. At every town we came to I got the latest edition of their newspaper, which invariably carried an item or two about Emmett. Despite the twenty-three bullet wounds in his body, he had made a miraculous recovery. He had been taken by train to the Montgomery County seat at Independence to be charged with the killings "by powder and leaden shot" of Cubine, Brown, Baldwin, and Connelly—even though it was clearly Bob who had pulled the trigger. Meanwhile, Ma and the rest of the family had signed away any and all legal rights to the estates of Robert and Grattan Dalton, even though notes were found on both bodies that their possessions should go to our mother in the event of death. The "estates" amounted to what was found on their bodies and, as reported by the newspapers, seemed a fairly accurate account of what I remembered each having on them—including their guns and Bob's nine hundred dollars in cash. It would all be probated by Judge Daniel Cline.

The good news, of course, was that Emmett had lived. Again I started plotting ways in which I could break him out of jail. The Montgomery County Jail could not be heavily defended, I believed, and just a few men—with the help of some strategically placed dynamite—could surely do the trick. . . .

In a week we had reached Garden City, where we stayed at the Ohio House for a few days, letting the horses rest up, posing as drovers and asking questions about business. Business was good, said a merchant by the name of John Curran, who was

staying at the Ohio House with us. Curran was a
funny sort of fellow, and I never knew what sort of
trade he was in, but he had a phenomenal memory
for names and faces—we only introduced ourselves
once, and hurriedly, but the next time he saw us he
called each of us by the phony name we had given.
Bitter Creek played poker with him once, and later
he said that Curran was a good card counter and
could keep track of what was left in the deck un-
commonly well. Even so, there is no accounting for
luck—Bitter Creek won more than two hundred dollars from him in one night, after which Curran's relationship with us cooled.

   Even though business was good, there seemed
to be more hardware stores than banks in Garden
City, so we moved on. As the days passed we drifted
back to the east, found nothing of interest in Lewis
or Kinsley, and made a wide berth around Dodge
City. On Halloween we arrived at Spearville, seventeen miles east of Dodge, in Ford County.

Six

We rode into Spearville from the north. Ol Yantis held the horses while Doolin, Bitter Creek, and I made for the front door of the Ford County Bank. By my watch it was precisely two o'clock in the afternoon.

We passed single file into the bank. I was strung tighter than a barbed-wire fence and I wished we were robbing another train. I gave one last look at the dirt-packed street, fought down an image of my blood soaking into it, then sucked in a lungful of winter air and followed the other two inside.

The bank was warm. The stove had been well tended.

There were two windows at the counter and Doolin went to one and began asking the cashier some questions about getting a loan. Bitter Creek went to the other counter. I lingered near the door to keep an eye on traffic and watch Yantis, who would signal us if trouble developed.

There was nobody in the bank except us, a cashier, and a clerk.

"Throw up your hands," Bitter Creek said as he

threw down on the clerk behind the window. "Throw them up damn quick, too."

The cashier dove behind the counter and began fumbling in his desk for a gun. Doolin grasped the top of the rail—which must have stood five feet from the ground—and in one leap swung himself over. It was the damnedest jump I ever saw. He landed on top of the luckless cashier, who went down in a heap under the outlaw's boots. Doolin took the revolver away from him and skidded it along the floor into a corner. Then he cocked his piece and held it to the cashier's head.

"Let's have no more of that," Doolin said. "There's no reason for anybody to get hurt. We're just here to conduct a little business—now, let's see about that loan."

"Yessir," the cashier said.

"Now that's more like it," said Doolin.

Doolin took a grain sack from inside his jacket and threw it on the cashier's desk. Bitter Creek had jumped over the counter, too, and was close to his man.

"Pile it all in there," he said. "Quick, you hear?"

The cashier began scooping banknotes into the sack.

I looked at my watch.

"One minute," I said.

I had drawn my revolver when Doolin had the trouble with the cashier, but now I put it back in its holster so nobody would think anything was wrong if they looked in. There wasn't a sign of any commotion on the street. Through the window, I could see that Yantis was leisurely smoking a cigar. Bitter Creek still had the drop on the other employee. The cashier kept filling the grain sack with money. I should have been feeling better now, but I wasn't. I felt like I was going to suffocate. I tugged at my collar to get more air down my neck. It had seemed pleasantly warm inside at first, but now it was downright hot.

"Is that all?" Doolin asked when the cashier had finished.

"Yessir," the cashier mumbled.

Doolin cocked the revolver again and pressed it to the man's forehead. He asked if he was sure.

"Well," the man said with eyes closed tight, "there's some silver here in the desk. I'll get it if you want it."

"I reckon so," Doolin said, and withdrew the gun. A red O the size of a dime shone on the cashier's high white forehead. He turned back to the desk and, under Doolin's watchful eye and ready gun, slowly opened a drawer. He began dipping handfuls of dollars into the grain sack.

My stomach was twisting up in knots. Two minutes had passed. I wanted to scream at the cashier to hurry up. I wanted to tell Doolin to get on with it. I was sure that folks were getting guns from the hardware store and fixing to blow us to pieces. Bullets would start pocking the windows at any moment. One of us would be hit and our iron would clatter to the floor, and it would be the beginning of a bloodbath that would end in a mad dash for the horses—

"Kid," Bitter Creek said.

I looked up.

"Are you okay?"

My Colt was cocked and ready in my shaking hand. Sweat poured down my face. I was losing my nerve in front of the men I respected most. I was nursing a yellow streak a mile wide. I recalled Emmett's mad ride back into death alley at Coffey-

ville to rescue Bob, already dying, and I wondered if
I would have as much sand facing certain death.

"You don't see anything out there, do you?" he
asked.

I pulled myself out of my morbid reverie and
looked out the window. There was a wagon rolling
down the street, with several men in rough-looking
clothes riding alongside. Deer carcasses were piled in
the back of the wagon.

"Yes," I said. "There's a hunting party coming
back into town."

Bitter Creek cursed.

Yantis had seen the hunters, too. He threw
down his cigar and mounted his horse. Still holding
the leads to the other horses, he began easing them
over toward the bank.

Doolin plucked the grain sack from the cashier.

"Gentlemen," he said, "it's time to leave."

Pushing the cashier in front of him, Doolin
started toward the front door. Bitter Creek backed
away from the other employee with his gun leveled.

The wagon had drawn to a stop about fifty
yards from the bank. The hunters had by now seen
that men with guns drawn were inside the bank, and
they began scrambling for their rifles stowed in the
bed of the wagon. I covered the gang while Doolin
and Bitter Creek swung up in their saddles.

"Much obliged," Doolin told the cashier, touching a forefinger to the brim of his hat. Then he
spurred his horse and Yantis and Bitter Creek followed.

When the first hunter came up from the wagon
with a rifle in his hands, I threw my Colt to eye level
and sent a round whistling over his head. He
dropped the gun and dove for cover. Then I put
three quick shots into the side of the wagon, making
splinters fly. The horses jumped and the wagon

lurched forward. The hunting party scattered, except for one rider on a paint who was trying to control his horse and shoulder his Winchester at the same time. He sent one wild shot into the ground near my left foot. While he was levering another round I mounted Cimarron, sent the last two shots in my gun in his direction, and tore off after the rest of the gang.

I reloaded on the fly, then looked at my watch—the entire job had taken less than three minutes. I also noticed, to my amazement, that my case of nerves had vanished when the action started.

The hunters quickly organized a posse and set out after us, but their horses were no match for ours. Only once did they get close enough to see us. We could hear the impotent popping of their rifles behind us—we were so far out of range that they must have been shooting just to make themselves feel better.

We made the Arkansas River Bottoms an hour or so before sundown, and there we stopped to divide the loot. There was seventeen hundred dollars, mostly in new five-dollar notes from the First National Bank of Dodge City. It worked out to four hundred and twenty-five dollars each, or a little more than a year's wages for your average cowboy—not exactly a fortune for risking your life, but a considerable amount of money.

Then we split up.

Seven

I had lots of time during the long ride back to the Territory and, as there wasn't the least sign of anybody on my trail, nothing to do but follow the stars and think.

At first I thought about the holdup, and I went over it so many times in my mind—especially the part where I laid down a withering cover fire so the gang could escape—that I wore it plumb out and got sick of it. Then I thought for a spell about how I could bust Emmett out of the Montgomery County Jail, but my mind seemed to stick on the part about how grateful Emmett would be, and I couldn't work up any decent escape plan—well, at least not one beyond simply blowing the living hell out of the jail with dynamite. That explosion kept getting bigger and bigger in my mind until it was unlikely to spare any living thing that had the misfortune to be in the jail building. Finally, along about midnight, I couldn't help but think about Lucky Lucinda, and I felt like somebody was poking around in my guts with a stick.

I told myself I didn't love her and I could count

off plenty of reasons: I had only spent one night with her, she had treated me like a dog the next morning, she was really not very pretty, and she was a whore—a sixteen-year-old whore, perhaps, and one who had been forced to a life of ill fame by the betrayal of a man she trusted, but a whore nonetheless. How could I care for a woman like that? Ma and her Bible would never allow it. From what I'd seen, it took a preacher's daughter to make a suitable mate for an outlaw. Look at Edith Ellsworth— she was the most proper lady you ever did see, and the most honest and true, and she was as devoted to Bill Doolin as the sun is to the morning. He never talked about his private business in her company, and she never asked. I expected those two to get hitched someday soon, and I was glad, although I was sort of scared for her, too; death was an ever-present possibility for an outlaw, particularly for one who was gaining as much notoriety as Doolin.

Why, just take Jesse James and his wife, Zerelda, as another example. Zerelda was his cousin and the finest woman who ever mourned for her slain outlaw. Zerelda was Jesse's mother's name, too, which gives it added effect. Do you think there would have been a ballad about Jesse if his wife had been a shameful whore? No, sir. This tradition goes all the way back to Robin Hood. Maid Marian was just that—a maiden—pure and unspoiled. How would it sound if it were Robin Hood and Marian, the whore?

As an outlaw, there was a certain standard I had to live up to when it came to women—at least marrying women—and the fact was that Lucinda was not even close to being outlaw wife material. I wasn't sure I knew any that were even close, with the obvious exception of Edith Ellsworth, and maybe Rose Dunn, but the fact that Rose wasn't a minister's daughter or locked up in a convent or suffering from a weak heart counted against her. Royal blood never hurt, neither.

When dawn came, I was exhausted from running all of this through my mind. I found myself in the Outlet, having crossed into the Territory sometime during the night, and I judged I was not far from the Cimarron River. Being in a fairly unpopulated stretch of land, I staked Cimarron out on the side of a little hillock and spread out my bedroll. I slept until midmorning, then ate a breakfast of hardtack and cold biscuits. Then I moved on.

I arrived back at Ingalls three days later, having moved slow and making sure that nobody was tracking me across the Outlet. I left Cimarron with Del Simmons, the boy at the livery, then walked down Ash Street to the restaurant run by Mrs. Thomas. I was about half-starved to death. I took a table by the window, where I had a good view of Ash and part of Second, and leaned my Winchester against the windowsill. I hung my hat from the top of the barrel.

Mrs. Thomas brought me a cup of coffee and I asked for an extra big order of bacon and eggs and plenty of hot bread. The coffee was the first warm thing I had tasted since before the Spearville job, partly because fires attract trouble and partly because I never could get the hang of camp cooking like my brother Emmett had. When I was nearly finished with my food I saw Lucinda coming west down Second Street from Sadie Comley's and I got that feeling in my gut again. She was carrying a basket and had on a calico dress and a bonnet that hid her face and she didn't look anything like a whore.

I watched as Lucinda came on down the street,

turned at the corner, and made for the restaurant. She apparently had been sent to pick up supper for the girls, and her head was down, so she didn't notice me sitting at the table when she walked in. She sat down at one of the tables in the back while she waited for Mrs. Thomas to load up the basket.

I put down my fork and thought things over and finally decided it wouldn't hurt just to say hello, to let her know I didn't harbor any bad feelings. So I walked over to her table and sat down.

"Do you mind some company?" I asked.

She looked at me and didn't say a word. She didn't have to. Her face, once I could see it plain, said it all. Her right eye was shining purple and nearly swollen shut, her cheeks were black and blue, and her bottom lip had been split

"Who did this to you?" I asked.

I couldn't imagine how anyone could bring themselves to strike a woman, much less beat the stuffing out of her—especially someone as small-boned as Lucinda, who could put up no more of a fight than a child could. But she wouldn't answer me. She just started crying, and the tears dripping from the swollen eye and rolling down her battered face almost made me cry, too.

"Please tell me," I said. "Was it a stranger? Was it somebody you knew?"

I put my hand on her shoulder but she shook me off.

"You don't understand," she said. "He'll kill me if I make any trouble for him. Please leave me alone."

I knew then who had beaten her. I squeezed her hand and returned to my seat by the window. Lucinda adjusted her bonnet, paid for the food Mrs. Thomas handed her, and gave me one last pleading look before she left.

I asked Mrs. Thomas if she knew where Darlington stayed when he was in town.

He wasn't at the O.K. Hotel. He had left that morning, Mrs. Pierce said, riding a sorrel mare. I found the horse hitched in front of Vaughn's saloon.

The saloon was little more than a tarpaper shack with sawdust on the floor but it had a real fancy bar. I walked in and laid my Winchester across the counter and asked for a shot of whiskey.

Charley Vaughn poured me one.

"What're you doing here, Kid?" he asked, putting the stopper back in the bottle. "I thought you were a regular over at old man Ransom's place."

"I got bored," I said.

I tried to pay for the whiskey, but Vaughn would not take my dime. I left the coins on the bartop anyway. There were seven or eight men in the saloon, most of them around a table in the corner, either playing poker or watching the game. The one with his back to the corner was wearing an expensive suit of clothes, black, with a derby hat. He was a big man, well muscled despite some fat, but handsome, with straight black hair and a black mustache. I could see how women fell for him. It was his turn to deal and he was shuffling cards and smoking a cigar.

"Darlington," I called.

The man in the suit did not look up. Instead, he put the cards aside and placed his hands palm down on the table. The others began moving out of the line of fire between Darlington and me.

"Only my friends address me by my last name without calling me mister," he said evenly. "I will give you the benefit of the doubt. Which one of my friends might you be?"

I stared at him.

"That's the Choctaw Kid," whispered one of his poker buddies.

"Do you intend to shoot an unarmed man?" Darlington asked. I have to admit that was my intention. "If you insist, will you at least do me the courtesy of telling me exactly what I am to die for?"

"You know damn well," I said.

"Oh," Darlington said, as if something had just come to him. "You must mean the affair with Lucky Lucinda. She did mention that you had become somewhat unreasonable after partaking of her charms. I assure you she is none the worse for wear, and quite used to my roughhousing—she would, in fact, worry that I didn't care if I left her without a reminder of our clinch."

I stared at him. My right hand was undecided between the Colt in its holster or the rifle on the counter. I was also watching his hands for any sign they were about to slap the butt of a shooting iron.

"Or perhaps it is the financial arrangement which you have come to question," Darlington said. "Not to worry—I paid Mrs. Comley in full for the time I spent with Lucinda. She is, after all, a common whore—she was mine to do with as I pleased. And it pleased me very much, while I poked her, to make her bleed."

Darlington pushed the table over with his legs and dove beneath it. I guessed I had only a fraction of a second to act before he came up shooting. My right hand snatched up the Winchester and I was in the corner and on top of him in an instant, swinging the rifle by the barrel like a baseball bat. Darlington was trying to bring a nickel-plated Smith & Wesson out of his boot with his left hand and the hammer had caught in the fabric of his pant leg. The stock of the rifle came down at the same time the barrel of the revolver came clear, and it struck with a mighty whack, smashing a couple of the fingers that were wrapped around the grip and sending the gun spinning out of his reach.

He stood there with blood dripping from his hand and hate burning in his eyes, daring me to kill him. And I should have sent a ball between his eyes right then. But Charley Vaughn called out for my guns so there would be no killing, and like a fool I tossed them over.

"You've shown that you can beat women," I said confidently. Somewhere I had heard, and unfortunately believed, that men who beat up women can't hold their own against another man. "Let's see what you can do against somebody who can fight back."

Darlington smiled.

"You ignorant bastard," he said, and sprang at me.

He hit me like a locomotive and drove me across the room into the counter. Bottles shook and crashed from the bar behind me. Even though the fingers of his left hand were broken, it didn't prevent him from making a fist and using his knuckles up and down my ribs and on my face. Finally I managed to get my right boot up against his stomach and pushed him away.

He came at me again, but this time I was on my feet and he led with a couple of rights and by this time it finally sank in that he was left-handed and I had to think reversed. The rights glanced off my forearm, and when he wound up for the pile-driver left there was an opening you could have driven a wagon through. He was strong, but he wasn't especially quick. I had done a fair job of trying to knock his front teeth down his throat before he even knew

I had connected, and he stood there for a moment swallowing blood and looking stupid.

But it lasted only a moment.

In the next second he was pounding at me again, and this time I was in trouble. One of his punches got through to my chin, rattling my teeth and making stars float in front of my eyes. There was a strange buzzing sound in my ears. I staggered, knocked over one of the tables, fell to my knees, and while I was down his fist slammed into my right ear, sounding like one of those explosions I hoped would someday level the Montgomery County Jail.

Then he kicked me in the ribs, and I heard something crack.

I fought the pain and struggled to my feet. I wasn't going to let him kick me to death. One more blow like that would lay me out for good. My eyes stung from the sweat and blood, and the right side of my head felt like it was numb and on fire at the same time. I could barely see Darlington in front of me. My hands hurt, as if I had driven the knuckles clear up to my wrists. I had never felt so tired. And what made my pain worse was the realization—the humiliation—that this beater of women was about to get the best of me, a Dalton.

I was glad that Grat was not here to see it.

Through my blurred eyes I saw a flash of silver. Darlington had pulled a knife, a big Arkansas pigsticker, from somewhere in the folds of his clothing. Suddenly my mind became sharp again, and I ignored the ringing in my ears. I became crazy mad, knowing I was about to fight for my life.

Vaughn told Darlington to drop the knife.

Darlington laughed.

I heard a double-barreled shotgun being cocked.

Darlington lunged forward, the blade in his left hand. Vaughn was behind us with the shotgun, but we were so close that he couldn't shoot one without hitting the other. I managed to block the knife with my left forearm.

I grasped his left wrist with my right hand and held it tightly against my forearm, then I began to pivot. The blade cut through my sleeve and found flesh, but it was so damned sharp—and I was so intent on getting the knife away from him— that I didn't feel it. Darlington grimaced in pain and cried out as his wrist was bent at an impossible angle. Blood from my arm spurted onto his face.

Finally his fingers lost their grip and the knife fell, landing point-first in the plank floor. Darlington was already half bent over, so I kicked him hard in the mouth. He went sprawling backward, howling in pain.

I snatched up the knife and landed with my knees on his chest.

Darlington coughed blood, turned his head, and spat out a tooth. I laid the already bloody edge of the pigsticker against his throat.

"Don't kill me," he gasped.

He hadn't needed to beg.

I tried to cut his throat, but once I had him down, I found that I couldn't kill him. My strength was fading fast and the room was growing dark. But I wanted to leave him with a clear reminder that he had lost this fight. So in one motion I slashed deeply across his face. He howled and clasped his hands over his face and writhed like a snake that's had its head cut off.

Then his hands fell away from his bloody face and his arms fell limply to the floor. I reckoned I had hurt him worse than I intended, because he wasn't moving and he wasn't breathing.

"Good God," Vaughn said. "You've killed him."

Then I collapsed in the blood and sawdust beside him.

Eight

They carried me to the O.K. Hotel and laid me in a bunk in the attic, where the cowboys slept. I was weak and bleeding something awful. They wrapped some rags around my arm and held them there while somebody went to fetch Doc Selph. When he finally arrived, he stitched up my arm and closed a gash over my right brow and generally cleaned me up. Then he gave me a big swallow of something he said would make me sleep, and I don't remember much after that.

Darlington's body, they told me later, had been thrown in the back of a wagon and driven off toward Stillwater by a couple of his poker-playing friends. They said his face—or rather, what was left of it—was one of the most gruesome things they had ever seen. I wasn't proud of what I had done to his face—it seemed in a way worse than killing somebody. I was glad that he had died.

Lucinda was there when I woke up that night. She was sitting in a chair by the side of the bunk, her hair down and falling around her shoulders, and the weak light of the kerosene lamp graciously concealed the bruises on her face. I tried to sit up, but couldn't.

"You better lie still," she told me. "Doc says you got a couple of busted ribs."

I believed her. It hurt every time I took a breath.

"Doc says you damn near bled to death."

"Well, damn near ain't the same *as*," I said, although I couldn't manage to sound confident about it. The exertion of talking made me cough, and coughing felt like somebody was grinding glass into my insides. When I had quieted down again, Lucinda took my hand and began rubbing it. I reckoned she was getting ready to say how grateful she was.

"Kid, that was really stupid," she said. "You nearly got yourself killed. I'm going to be healed up in a few days and you're going to be wheezing around for weeks. Why did you try to give Darlington a fair fight? You should have shot him dead when you had the chance, instead of giving him the opportunity to work you over. I know—he's been working me over for years. You're lucky you killed him, because he would have been twice as dangerous left alive."

She squeezed my hand.

"If you wanted to do something for me, why didn't you bring me flowers or buy me chocolates or in any way treat me like a human animal instead of a whore? Fighting over me made me feel like property."

I sighed—long, low, and carefully.

Lucinda was right, of course. My own expectations of how the world works—that the world should somehow be *fair*—had nearly done me in again.

"Besides," she said, and tears began to roll down her cheeks, "I knew he would hurt you and I didn't want that. I kept waiting for you to come back so I could apologize for the way I had treated you that morning. Don't you see that I was mean on purpose? I was trying to chase you away, because I was really starting to care about you, and whores can't afford to care. It's too painful."

Something swelled up in my chest that wasn't pain. I turned my hand over and laced my fingers into hers. If I had been well enough I would have scooped her up into my arms. Everything I had told myself on the trail about Lucinda were lies, and the one true thing I had not been able to admit until now. Despite the pain my body was in, that hole in the middle of my soul didn't hurt any longer.

The knife wound left an angry red scar on my forearm, and my ribs eventually knitted. Toward the end of November I was able to ride again, and Doolin suggested that we pay a visit to Yantis at his sister's place near Orlando. Bitter Creek came along as well, because Doolin figured we might pull a job or two after collecting Ollie.

We arrived at the sister's cotton farm the evening of December 2, and we could tell right away there was something wrong. No smoke was coming from the chimney, and there was no activity nor any other sign that the farm was a going concern. We hitched our horses and stepped up onto the front porch. The front door was standing wide-open and everything was dark inside.

Doolin walked into the house.

"Ollie?" he called.

It was quiet for a moment, then a sad voice said: "He ain't here."

"Mrs. McGinn?" Doolin asked.

"Yeah."

"It's Bill Doolin and Bitter Creek and the Kid," he said. "What're you doing sitting alone in the dark?"

"Deathwatch," she said.

It was as cold as hell in the house—much colder, in fact, than it was outside.

Bitter Creek lit a match on his boot heel and held it up until he spotted a lamp on the table. Then he took the globe off and touched the match to the wick. The flame grew and illuminated the room. In the center was a coffin with the lid off. Bitter Creek moved the lamp over to look inside. Ollie Yantis was laid out there, with silver dollars over his eyes.

There was a mirror and a clock on the fireplace mantel. The pendulum of the clock had been stopped and the mirror had been turned to face the wall.

"You shouldn't be here," she said. "The law's been here looking for you."

Mrs. McGinn was old, probably near forty, and a widow. She wore an old blue dress with a black band pinned to one sleeve. Oliver had been her only living relative. In her lap was a big Schofield revolver—cocked.

"We'll sit with you for a spell," Doolin said, with just the right amount of sympathy in his voice. "Bitter Creek, won't you gather the horses and take them somewhere around back, close to the kitchen door?"

Bitter Creek nodded.

Doolin took a seat near Mrs. McGinn and looked at me. I was standing near the front door, still staring at the coffin.

"You don't feel like leaving, do you?" Doolin asked.

I shook my head.

"Then see if you can build us a fire. It's power-ful cold."

There were some logs and a box of kindling by the fireplace, so I began making a fire. While I worked I listened as Doolin talked to the widow.

"Won't you give me that hogleg?" Doolin asked.

She made no effort to hand the gun over.

"Tell us what happened," Doolin said gently.

"They killed him," she said.

"Yes, we know. Tell us *how* it happened."

"A few days ago Ham Hueston, a city marshal from Stillwater, came out to see us with a fellow from Garden City named Curran. Did you know this Curran?"

"Yes," Doolin said.

"Well, this Curran fellow said he was a horse buyer and inquired if we had any horses to sell. Of course, we didn't, but Oliver told them of some neighbors that might, and they thanked us and rode off. Oliver was very upset by this visit, but he would not tell me why. He just said he had to leave, and he planned to take off the next day, the twenty-eighth.

"It was heavy fog that morning. The officers hid their horses at a neighbor's farm and walked over to our place on foot. They took up positions between the house and the barn. There was four of them: Tom Hueston and his brother, Hamilton, and their friend George Cox, and a sheriff from Dodge City."

"Chalk Beeson?"

"Yes, that's the name. A strange name, isn't it?"

She stared into the fire, which was bursting to life in the fireplace.

"Tell us what happened next."

"At daybreak Oliver went out the back door to feed the horses," she said. "He was wearing a pistol in a holster under his armpit, and he was carrying a feed bag in one hand. I had breakfast nearly made, and I watched him from the kitchen window. The fog was so thick it looked like cotton. You couldn't see a thing. He was just a few steps out the door when somebody hollered for him to stop. Oliver dropped the feed bag and fired at the voice. Then guns opened up from everywhere. There were bullets hitting the house and breaking windows. Oliver had been shot and he was on the ground, but he was still shooting back and he told them to go right to hell. Those were his exact words: 'Go right to hell.'

"I rushed out the back door to him. He was bleeding badly, but he was still holding on to his gun. I screamed at the marshals to stop killing him. . . . The sheriff said they had no intention of killing him if Oliver would just give up his gun and surrender. So I pleaded with Oliver, and he finally gave me his gun and I gave it to the sheriff. He was so bad off, I don't think he could have held on to it much longer. He couldn't move from the waist down. The bullet had struck him just above the hip on his right side and broke his spine.

"Well, they put some bandages around him and loaded him up in our wagon and took him to Orlando. They put him in a hotel room and got a doctor for him, but Oliver died at one o'clock that afternoon. I was with him at the end. The sheriff took his wallet and said the five-dollar notes were from a bank robbery at Spearville, Kansas. I said I didn't know anything about it. After they laid him in the coffin and took a picture of him, they let me put him back in the wagon and bring him home."

I crouched by the fire, waiting for her to continue. Bitter Creek came in through the back and sat down on the other side of Mrs. McGinn.

"Is that all?" Doolin asked.

"Why don't you ask what you mean?" she said, with more than a little anger in her voice, and I suddenly became acutely aware of the cocked gun in her lap. "Did Oliver identify his partners in the Spearville robbery? No, he did not. I want you boys to know that he died game, that he was cursing those officers to the end, and that he made absolutely no admissions or confessions."

Doolin nodded.

"I'm sorry, ma'am," he said, "but we had to ask."

"You can go now," she said. "The officers keep asking me and the neighbors about men visiting the farm on good racing stock, and it wouldn't surprise me if they weren't hiding outside waiting to kill you, too."

"Mrs. McGinn, do you have anyone to help you bury Oliver?"

She looked down at her lap.

"I didn't want him in the ground yet. That's why I've been sitting here in the cold and the dark, to keep him cool and stretch things out a bit. I haven't slept since bringing him home. I've been watching over him, like I used to. He's my baby brother. . . ."

She began to sob, terrible spasms that shook her frail body, and Doolin gently reached over and took the gun from her lap. He told Bitter Creek to stay inside and try to get her into bed if he could, and he motioned for me to come out back with him. We went out the back door toward the barn, and I suddenly felt as if a hundred rifles were trained on me. I had a roll of those same five-dollar First National Bank of Dodge City notes in *my* pocket.

We found a shovel and a pick in the barn. By lantern light we began digging a grave in what seemed the prettiest corner of the yard out back. It was slow going. The ground was frozen and we had to break through the crust with the pick. We stopped for coffee a couple of times to warm us up, and Bitter Creek spelled me once, and by dawn we had it finished.

Mrs. McGinn watched while we nailed down the lid and carried the coffin out and lowered it down into the hole. The fog had rolled in pretty thick and it was spooky standing around the grave.

"I'm not much for making up prayers," Doolin said, "but as leader of this gang I feel I should say a word or two. I can't say anything fancy or literary, because I never learned to read or write anything but my own name. But Oliver was a good boy, and he never killed anybody that I ever heard about, and he was the truest partner you could ever hope for. If he had a failing, it was bad companions, and God should take that into account. Oh, and he was lucky to have a sister that loved him a bunch, because some folks go through this world without ever having anybody care for them. Amen."

Then we filled up the grave and Mrs. McGinn went inside and slept. We tucked the covers around her and made sure the fire was well banked and the doors secure. Then we rode out while the fog was still on the ground.

Nine

After burying Yantis, things began to change for the Wild Bunch. We became more cautious. We put off another job until things quieted down a bit. On the way back to Ingalls we rode mostly at night. We became married to our Winchesters, eating and sleeping with them, and always making sure they had full magazines. Our six-guns were important, too, but in a desperate fight with a posse it would be the carbines with their longer range, greater accuracy, and more shots before reloading that would make all the difference. We began carrying as much ammunition as possible in our saddlebags, sometimes a couple hundred rounds or more. We were preparing for nothing less than a small war.

It didn't come, at least not right away. There was still some sand left in the glass for us.

Chalk Beeson may have suspected that Doolin and Bitter Creek were involved in the Spearville robbery, but he could not march Mr. Curran of Garden City into the Ransom and Murray Saloon at Ingalls for a positive identification, so there was no warrant out for them. As for me, nobody knew me by my real name, and I had not been linked, under any name, to Doolin and the others. For the time being, I was simply—as the newspapers reported—"one fair-complexioned man, of medium height and weight" riding a "small chestnut horse of apparent racing stock." That could describe just about anybody, and a good many horses.

After getting back to Ingalls, the first place I visited was Sadie Comley's. While on the trail I had thought of little besides Lucinda, even when I should have been worrying about posses and warrants. It was strange, but seeing Yantis stretched out in a coffin in the parlor of his sister's house had made me melancholy in the worst way—the grave seems terribly lonely, and we are all headed there, no matter which route we take, and for me the only way of easing the awful anticipation of that loneliness was to be physical with someone that mattered. For some folks, I guess, religion holds some comfort— my ma, in particular, was a believer—but from what I'd seen, religion was just fairy tales to make living folks feel better about the dead. For me, I always felt a lot closer to the great mystery in a whorehouse than in a church—well, at least when I was with Lucinda. I wanted her in the most desperate, love-sick way. I missed the way she smelled and the way she fit into my arms and the little animal sounds she made. I especially missed the things she did with her mouth, for which there are simply no words to describe. I also had some notion that since I had declared my affection for her, Lucinda would give up whoring.

Bitter Creek and I had rode into town together that first morning back, and as I reined Cimarron to a halt in front of Sadie's, he grinned broadly beneath his mustache.

"Are you going to visit that little whore of yours?" Bitter Creek asked.

I bristled, but Bitter Creek was just stating the facts. I allowed that perhaps I would visit Lucinda, not wanting to betray the depth of my feelings to a saddlemate who would find in it a source of endless amusement.

"Good," he said. "You've been thinking so hard about her on the trail that I'm plumb wore out from listening to it. See you at the saloon."

Then he laughed and rode on.

I hitched Cimarron out front and walked around Mrs. Comley's house to the back. The window to Lucinda's room was down, but not latched, and I slid it up and stepped up into the house. Then I shut the window behind me and sat down on the edge of the bed.

Lucinda was asleep. I nudged her until she finally roused and sat up. It took her a moment to recognize me.

"Kid," she said, and smiled. She leaned forward and kissed me on the cheek. "When did you get back?"

"Just now. I wanted to talk to you."

"About what?" she asked.

"About us, of course."

I told her as best I could about the death of Ollie Yantis and digging his grave in the middle of the night and how it had got me thinking. I even told her about when I felt most religious, although I didn't know if she would understand. She smiled through most of it, but when I finally got around to the part about her retiring and us getting married, her face clouded over.

"No," she said.

"What do you mean?" I asked.

"I mean no," she said. "I'm not giving up my

tricks for you, not unless you agree to give up the outlaw trail for me. Are you willing to do that?"

"I don't know anything else," I said.

"Well, I don't know anything else, either," she said. "I may be a whore, but at least I have my own money and I run my life, not some man. Maybe in time I can manage to save up a little money and get into something better, but for right now this is all I've got, and it's stable. If I quit this and throw in with you—and then you don't quit the gang—it'll just be a matter of time before somebody rides into town to tell me about how they dug your grave after Chalk Beeson or somebody like him tracked you down. I love you, Kid, but no thanks."

I must have looked pretty disappointed.

"Don't take it so hard," she said, and put her arms around my shoulders. "I don't even know what your real name is. But we still have our time together. Let's enjoy each other while we can. You do enjoy me, don't you?"

She kissed me, long and slow. She tasted as good as I remembered, and I kicked off my boots and began shucking my clothes. I hated the idea of her being with other men for money, but I hated the idea of being without her worse.

Afterward I took Cimarron to the livery and gave the boy, Del Simmons, a silver dollar to take good care of him. Then I trudged down the street toward the saloon with my Winchester slung over my shoulder. It was a bitter cold day and my breath billowed before me. When I passed Widow McMurtry's notions shoppe—that's the way she spelled it—I had to stop for a moment and stare at the window, which she had cleverly decorated for Christmas. There was a little evergreen tree with candles and angels and sparkling ornaments. Wooden toys and cherubic paper dolls danced around the base of the tree. I was standing there stone still, staring like an idiot at a toy gun like one I'd had as a kid, when I felt someone behind me.

I spun around with the business end of the Winchester at waist level.

"You don't want to shoot me, Sam."

It was my brother Bill. He was dressed in a dark suit with a telltale bulge beneath the left arm. His hat was pulled low over his eyes, and when he lifted his hat in a gesture of greeting, I saw that his hair was streaked with gray. He looked older and thinner than I remembered.

I lowered the rifle.

"What in hell are you doing here?" I asked.

"I've come to talk to Doolin," he said.

I stopped in my tracks.

"What in hell for?" I asked.

He wouldn't answer me.

"Well, this is the place," I said. "You can probably find him in the saloon. Come along, for that's where I'm headed."

Bill nodded and fell into step.

"Looks like the world is treating you well," he said, but his tone of voice sounded as if he were more interested in making conversation than in finding out how I really was.

"I'm still kicking," I said. "How's Jenny and the kids?"

"Good," he said. "They are coming to Kingfisher to live with Ma."

Doolin and Bitter Creek were sitting at their usual table at the Ransom and Murray Saloon. Doolin had a shot of whiskey in front of him.

"This here's Bill Dalton," I said.

My brother offered his hand, but Doolin just

nodded. Bitter Creek touched a finger to the brim of his hat.

We sat down with them.

Doolin looked Bill up and down and took a sip of his whiskey. "I thought you were a senator or some other kind of high-and-mighty politician out yonder in California," he said. "What are you doing in the Territory?"

"Well, I did have political ambitions," Bill said. "But the thing was, after my brothers were wrongly accused of robbing so many banks and trains, everything went sour for me. Folks didn't want a politician with the last name of Dalton. After Coffeyville, it was hopeless. . . ."

"So what are you doing here?" Doolin asked again.

"I want to join up."

"With the Wild Bunch?"

"Yes, sir."

"What in hell for?" I asked, now for the second time.

"Gold and glory," he said. "And revenge."

"You'll get yourself killed," I said.

"Look who's talking."

Doolin held his hand up between us.

"There's room in this gang for only one leader," Doolin said, "and I'm it. Your brother Bob and I sometimes went head-to-head on some things with the old gang, and I know where that shoe pinches."

"I don't want to lead," Bill said, so earnestly that I believed him. "I don't have the qualifications. Why, I've never robbed a bank or a train in my life—in fact, I've never robbed so much as a candy store, and that's the truth. But I am pretty handy with a shooting iron, and like all Daltons, I have more nerve than sense. I aim to make the banks and railroads bleed for what they did to my brothers,

Mr. Doolin, and I will do it with or without your help."

"That's a pretty speech," Doolin said. "But how do I know that you haven't been sent down here by Chalk Beeson or some other fool pinned to a tin star?"

Bill reached inside his jacket.

Doolin and Bitter Creek pulled their six-guns and had them cocked and aimed at Bill's head before he even got his hand all the way inside his jacket.

"Take it easy," my brother said.

"Mister," Bitter Creek said, "don't ever do that again. I damn near blowed your head clean off."

Slowly now, Bill pulled some papers from his inside jacket pocket. He held them out for Doolin to inspect.

"Give it to the Kid," Doolin said, regarding the papers as if they were a ball of snakes.

I took them. The top one was a postcard sent by Sheriff Chalk Beeson advising of a reward for information about the Spearville job.

"Says here that the Ford County Bank is offering a four-hundred-and-fifty-dollar reward for information leading to our capture," I told Doolin. "Of course, it doesn't identify us by name, just gives descriptions of four men. They aren't even very good descriptions—none use the word *dashing* or *daring*. 'Robbers have large number new five-dollar bills issued by First National Bank, Dodge City, Kansas.' "

"So that's why Curran found the courage to finger Ollie," Doolin remarked sadly.

"Look at the other one," Bill said.

It was a handwritten list of times, dates, and places.

"It's a train schedule."

"It's more than that," Bill said. "It's a list of all of the big Santa Fe payrolls for the next six months.

It was given to me by someone in a position to know."

"And why would they give it to you?" Doolin asked.

"Because an unfairly treated employee knew I would use the information to strike back against the railroads. The battle of Mussel Slough is still fresh in the memory of many of those in Tulare County, Mr. Doolin, and it is common knowledge that I have been persecuted by the railroads for speaking out against their monopolies, monopolies that are breaking the back of the common man."

"Well, I am not interested in becoming a martyr for the grangers," Doolin said. He took the handwritten schedule from me and tucked it inside his vest. "But good information is hard to find. Let me keep this for a spell, and if it pans out, you're in."

My brother was silent.

By the look on his face, I could tell that Doolin's decision was not what he had hoped for.

"I want to ride with you," he said, "like my brothers."

"Look here," Doolin said. "How do I know that you ain't setting us up? We could be walking into an ambush instead of a payroll. Besides, if your information is good, you can be a more important part of the gang by getting us *more* intelligence than by riding with us and risking your hide. You can keep us informed on what the law and the railroads are doing to catch us."

My brother nodded.

"There's just one thing," he said. "When the gang is ready for the big casino, the one job that is bigger than all the rest, I want to be there. I want to board that train with a gun in my hand and ride off with a fortune. I don't want to be left holding the bag after the rest of the gang has lit out for South America, or wherever it is outlaws retire now."

Doolin studied his face for a moment.

"Fair enough," Doolin said, and they shook hands.

Later I asked my brother to walk down to the Thomas Restaurant and eat supper with me. He was a little moody, but agreed. I had always considered Bill one of my good brothers—like Frank was—and I did not want him to take the owlhoot trail. We ate in silence, and when we were sipping coffee afterward I spoke.

"I thought you were too smart for this," I told him.

"Sometimes smart isn't enough."

"Then you must want to get yourself killed."

"They won't kill me."

"Are you somehow luckier than Bob or Grat?"

"Are you?" he asked.

"That's different," I said. "I'm going to do this just long enough to save enough money and . . ."

"And what?"

"Well, here's the thing," I said, leaning toward him. "I plan to bust Emmett out of the Montgomery County Jail. I can't abide the idea of him spending the rest of his life behind bars. If you want to see some action, then why don't you help me with Em?"

"Whoa," Bill said. "What gives you the idea that he's going up for life?"

"Are you kidding?" I asked. "Em's been charged with the murders of Cubine and Brown. They aren't going to let him off with a slap on the wrist. Those folks in Coffeyville would lynch him if they could get away with it."

Bill shook his head.

"The prosecutor has offered to recommend a sentence of ten to fifteen years if Emmett will plead guilty. Now, there's no guarantee of what Judge McCue will do, but a prosecutor's recommendation is usually followed."

"Fifteen years?" I asked.

"Emmett would be in his thirties," Bill said. "That wouldn't be too bad for him, would it?"

"No," I said, "but how can we be sure?"

"We can't. But it would be a shame to try and bust Emmett out if he was going to get ten years instead of life. How were you planning on doing it—blowing a hole in the side of the jail or mounting some type of assault? Even Quantrill only tried taking a brick building once, then said he'd had his fill. Hell, the penalty for breaking jail is probably more than *that*. Let's wait. Emmett's got a good attorney—I trust him."

Bill was funny that way about politicians and attorneys.

He finished his coffee and asked, "What should I tell Ma?"

"About what?"

"About you," he said. "She doesn't know if you're alive or dead. She says she hasn't heard a word from you, and she can't ask for fear of fingering you for the Coffeyville raid—even if nobody does know your real name."

I twisted up a quirly, then passed the makings to Bill. We smoked about half of our cigarettes while I thought of what to say. The problem was that I kept imagining how to tell Ma that I was in love with a prostitute.

"Don't tell her anything," I said at last.

We parted on somewhat warmer terms than we had met. I was still against him joining the gang, but he agreed to stick to gathering information if I would put off busting Emmett out of jail, at least until he was sentenced. But Bill still held out for the big casino, the last and greatest job. It wasn't until Bill was on his way back to Kingfisher that I realized what the really important difference was between him and Bob and Grat, and what I should have told him: they didn't have families to leave behind.

"I've got something for you, Mr. Doolin."

The stocky man with the thick red mustache and tousled hair stood expectantly before us. He was hatless and his clothes were not much more than rags. His bright, sharp eyes darted between Doolin, Bitter Creek, and myself. We were seated at our usual table at the Ransom and Murray Saloon in Ingalls, and we had known for twenty minutes that he was coming—one of the Pickering boys had told us that a stranger leading six horses was riding bareback into town.

Doolin didn't say anything at first, but just sat staring at the rascal. When he had decided that the sorry apparition before us posed no threat—there didn't seem to be anywhere on his body to hide a gun or a writ—the outlaw chief asked his name.

"Waightman," he answered quickly. "Red Buck to my friends."

"All right," Doolin said. "I'm game. What do you have for me?"

Red Buck walked toward the door and motioned for us to follow.

Outside, tied to one lead, were seven horses. They ranged from moderate to good in appearance and would make fine mounts. None of the horses had saddles. The stranger had apparently ridden the lead horse bareback, and used what looked like a piece of clothesline for the others. The lead and some of the other horses had bits and bridles, but most simply had the line wrapped awkwardly around their heads. It was a wonder the horses hadn't stamped him to death or torn him to pieces.

"I'm a horse thief," Red Buck said.

"So it seems," Doolin said.

"These are for you—for your gang."

"What's the deal?" Doolin asked suspiciously.

"Let me join. I want to be part of your gang."

Doolin sniffed and tugged at his mustache. His expression said, *My God, they're crawling out of the woodwork today.*

"I don't know you," he said. "You could be anybody, including a federal marshal sent here to infiltrate the gang. Even if you're not, I don't know if you can be trusted."

"I've heard of this man," Bitter Creek said. "He was arrested a couple of years ago for stealing some mules in the Cherokee Nation. He was sentenced to the federal prison at Detroit."

"Is this true?" Doolin asked.

The man nodded.

"Why are you out of prison so quickly?" Bitter Creek asked.

"I escaped from the prison train as it left Lebanon, Missouri," Red Buck said. "I've been hiding out since, but it has been a rough life. After hearing about Bill Doolin and his gang, I reckoned that was the place I ought to be."

"Mules?" I asked. "You went to prison for stealing mules?"

He shrugged. "Some people like mules."

"How'd you find us?" Doolin asked.

The eyes darted around again.

"I've been asking questions all over the Creek Nation. Folks told me that the Dunn brothers ran a traveler's rest along the Cimarron, so I went there. After considerable hemming and hawing—and after I gave him a horse—Bee Dunn told me to come here."

Doolin looked at me and then Bitter Creek. I shrugged and Bitter Creek turned his hands outward in a "why not?" gesture.

"Okay," Doolin said, "you are a probationary member of the Wild Bunch. You watch how we do things and try to get in step."

"Yessir."

"There is to be no robbing or thieving unless it is okayed by me, and there is to be no trouble here in Ingalls. These people depend on us for the money we bring into town, and we depend on them for watching our backsides while we're here. You didn't steal those horses around here, did you?"

"No, sir."

Doolin took out his poke and peeled a couple of ten-dollar notes from the roll. He started to give the money to Red Buck, then suddenly pulled back his hand.

"You're not a drunk, are you?"

Red Buck shook his head.

"Good," Doolin said, and gave him the money. "Take the horses over to the livery yonder and get them squared away. Then go buy yourself some decent clothes over at Beal's store. Nothing flashy, but something that will wear well. Don't worry about shooting irons—we have plenty and will fix you up. You might also get yourself a bath and a haircut."

We watched as he walked the horses away.

"Boys," Doolin said, "what do you think?"

"I think we are in trouble if Bee Dunn would sell us out in exchange for a horse. We had better talk to that man," Bitter Creek said. Then: "Do you always have to adopt people so?"

"Well," Doolin said sulkily, "we can use the horses."

"Thank God he wasn't leading mules," I said.

Ten

The guns of Coffeyville and the killing of Yantis became only bitter memories as the Christmas of 1892 approached. The Wild Bunch was larger and stronger than ever; in addition to the big jobs, which were carried out by Doolin and his lieutenants (of which I was one), there was a more or less constant trade in stolen horses and whiskey carried on by the lesser gang members. It got so that I could scarcely count the number of people that were on the Wild Bunch payroll. Business was so brisk that, for Doolin, going to the Ransom and Murray Saloon was like reporting for work.

One afternoon in mid-December Doolin was playing poker with me and Bitter Creek when the door to the saloon flew open and a sorry-looking fellow came tearing up to the table. His chest heaved and sweat rolled down his cheeks, even though it was freezing outside.

No sooner had he crossed the room to the bar than the door opened again. A slim young man walked a couple steps into the room and planted his feet, his thumbs hooked on his gun belt. He was a clean-shaven fellow and his neat clothes and well-shined boots said he was a lawman.

"Come peaceful," the young fellow said. "Don't make me trail you any farther in this miserable weather."

The ragged fellow scurried over to our table.

"Bill," he pleaded with Doolin. "I've come to join up—don't let them arrest me."

A look of horror crossed the lawman's face as he realized who Doolin was. Doolin ignored them both, played out his hand, and watched disgustedly as Bitter Creek raked in his money.

Then he asked the lawman: "Who are you?"

"I'm—" He stopped and tugged at his collar, and I could tell he was thinking about lying, then decided against it. He must have been new and green or he wouldn't have come into the saloon— much less Ingalls—in the first place. "I'm Payne County Deputy Sheriff Bob Andrews and I've got a warrant for the arrest of that man."

"Don't let him take me—"

"Shut up, will you?" Doolin said. "What's he done?"

"He knocked an old man in the head with a brick and stole forty dollars. The old man damn near died."

Doolin considered this bit of information.

"What do you say, Bill? Will you take me in?" the ragged man asked.

Doolin shook his head.

"No, I won't. Anybody that would knock an old man in the head for forty dollars isn't fit to carry water for this bunch."

Doolin drew his revolver and told Bitter Creek to relieve the fugitive of his gun. It was an old Remington in a rotting holster that had more cracks

and splits than it did leather. Bitter Creek offered the
gun to Doolin.

"No, give it to the sheriff. Boys, we're going to
take a little ride with this young man. If we don't,
he's liable to get potted before he gets out of town."

We fetched the horses from the livery and escorted Andrews and his prisoner out of town. About
five miles down the Stillwater Road, Doolin called
for us to halt.

"I reckon this is far enough," Doolin said.
"Sheriff, I'm going to take you on your word that
you won't cross us. If you do—well, we'll meet
again."

Doolin touched a finger to the brim of his hat
and we rode back to Ingalls.

Folks was always crawling in off the trail and
asking Doolin for work—legal or otherwise—but I
remember the story of the ragged man best because
it shows just what type of person Doolin was: a gentleman who also happened to be an outlaw.

The more time I spent with Lucinda, the more I began to realize that she was a person, too, no worse
and probably a damn sight better than most of us.
When I was with her it was easy to forget about her
profession—there didn't seem to be room for anything in the world except her—but when we were
apart I brooded on it some. I still wanted her to quit
whoring, but things didn't seem so black and white
anymore.

I had quite a poke of money from the jobs the
gang had pulled, and I used a little of it to buy
Lucinda presents—ribbon and lace and paper things,
some jewelry, clothes. It never felt right buying
things for myself—I still wore the same buckskin
shirt and black hat, and the Colt with the beaded

holster, that I'd had for what seemed like forever—but buying for her was different. She loved presents and her enthusiasm for boxes done up in brown paper and twine was like that of a child. She would clap her hands and shake the boxes and try to guess what was in them. She loved toys, and I bought her a whole family of dolls from McMurtry's shop.

Her face had healed up nicely, and her spirit had seemed to mend as well. I took her for long rides in the country, and we would have picnic lunches deep in the woods, away from the frowns of the respectable folks in Ingalls.

A country dance was held the Saturday before Christmas at Ed Williams's log house, a couple of miles west of Ingalls. The Meyers boys fiddled and called, and there was a guitar or two, and Old Man Williams had the windows hung with burlap because Doolin was afraid somebody might take a potshot at him from outside. Doolin furnished store-bought oysters and salt crackers, which was a treat for most folks at the party, because cash was hard to come by.

Doolin was more slicked up than I'd ever seen him. He wore a dark suit and vest, and his reddish-brown hair was combed straight back and his black mustache was trimmed real good. He walked into the dance with Edith Ellsworth on his arm, and although I never considered her much of a looker, she turned heads that night. Part of it was her white store-bought dress and part of it was the way she seemed to glow—she positively radiated happiness.

She and Doolin danced a couple of tunes, then Doolin shushed the musicians and asked for everybody to hold it down because he had an announcement to make.

"I guess you all know me," Doolin said, holding Edith's hand. "You've been mighty good to me and my boys. I don't think there's anyplace on earth where I would feel more welcome. That's why I'm proud to share my good fortune with you tonight. . . . Miss Edith Ellsworth of Ingalls, Oklahoma Territory, has agreed to be my wife."

The men whooped and hollered and a crowd of well-wishers formed around Doolin and his bride-to-be. The men pumped Doolin's hand and the ladies all seemed to talk to Edith at once, and it all made for quite a racket. I hung back because I couldn't believe what I had heard—how on earth was Doolin going to juggle being a husband while leading Oklahoma Territory's most notorious bunch of outlaws? It just didn't make much sense to me; you can't run a gang of desperadoes and go home to your wife, and possible children, at five o'clock. It didn't wash. Do you tell the posse closing in on you, "Sorry, but I have to go home now. The little woman is holding supper."

I was so mad that my hands were shaking and my cheeks were hot. Bitter Creek had a pint of whiskey hidden in his coat and I made him give it to me and I downed it, right there on the spot.

Then I went outside and rolled myself a quirly and sat on a stump and smoked it. I was considering riding into Ingalls and making them open up the saloon or the drugstore so I could get some more liquor when Bitter Creek came out. He put a boot up on my stump and leaned on his knee.

"What's up, hoss?"

"Nothing," I said.

"Well, you're acting like it's something. How come you're riled with Doolin for plighting his troth to Edith?"

"It don't seem right," I said.

"Why not?"

I didn't have a good answer.

"Well," Bitter Creek said, "maybe you're not really mad at Doolin at all. Maybe—just maybe—you're angry because you can't announce *your* engagement to your little ... to your girl. Do you think that could be it?"

I flicked my butt away.

"I don't know," I said.

But I was lying—I *did* know, and Bitter Creek had hit the nail on the head.

"You're right," I confessed. "I can't marry Lucinda—I can't even take her to a dance like this, not with these good folks around."

"Look here, Kid," Bitter Creek said. "You don't have to impress anybody here, except maybe me and Doolin, and you know you're square with us. I reckon a fallen dove is as much of an outlaw as we are. So go get Lucky and bring her back, if that's what would make you two happy. Say to hell with what anybody else thinks."

"You think it'd be all right?"

"Who do you think makes the rules around here?" Bitter Creek asked, pulling back his jacket to reveal the butt of his revolver.

I rode straight into town and let Cimarron's reins fall on the ground outside Lucinda's window. I slid the window up and stepped in and about scared the living daylights out of a fat gent who had just dropped his suspenders.

He grabbed his wallet and held it close to his chest.

"Don't worry," I said. "I ain't going to rob you."

"Kid," Lucinda said. "What're you doing here?"

"Put your best dress on," I told her. "We're going to the dance tonight."

She stared at me like I was out of my mind.

"You heard me," I said. "Do you want to go or don't you?"

She hugged me and started dressing.

"Just wait a minute," the fat man said. "I paid three dollars for a poke, and I aim to have it."

I pressed a five-dollar note into his hand.

"Mister, you made a profit tonight," I said. "You just go back out there and pick another of Sadie's girls, because this young lady is otherwise engaged for the rest of the night."

I pushed him out the door and threw his shoes and jacket after him. When Lucinda was dressed we slipped out the window and we rode double back to the Williams place.

When we walked inside things got real quiet all of a sudden. The music stopped and everybody turned to look. Then the whispers began. Several of the men looked uncomfortable, and I wondered how many of them had visited her at Sadie Comley's place. The women, especially the wives, looked downright hateful. Doolin and Bitter Creek were standing together, and they looked questioningly at me. I shook my head. It kind of spoils things if you have to make someone feel welcome at the point of a gun.

Lucinda's face turned bright red and she stared at her toes.

"Come on, Kid," she said. "Take me back where I belong."

Then Edith Ellsworth left her group of women friends and strode briskly across the floor toward us. Lucinda turned, not wanting to face the tirade that she thought was coming from a preacher's daughter.

Edith laid a hand gently on Lucinda's forearm.

"That's a lovely dress," she said. "Did you make it?"

"No," Lucinda stammered. "The Kid bought it for me."

"Well, it's simply wonderful. I'm so glad you came. Do come along and have some punch—Kid, you don't mind if I steal her for a little while?—I've got wonderful news to share with you. Bill and I are getting married come March. We'd love to have you and the Choctaw Kid at the ceremony. You know, Bill thinks so highly of him. . . ."

The gossiping had stopped and everybody was watching Edith and Lucinda, and Edith was going on as if there was nothing at all unusual about a town prostitute attending a country dance. I was beginning to understand what it was that Doolin loved about this tall, bucktoothed, plain-looking girl.

Bitter Creek walked over to the musicians and said, "Play!"

He didn't have to tell them twice. Soon there were couples on the floor dancing again, and people chatting and generally enjoying themselves. A few folks stomped out because of Lucinda, but not many.

Lucinda and I danced so much that night my dashboards were plumb wore out. Lucinda also danced with Doolin and Bitter Creek and a couple of fellows I didn't even know. When dawn came, and the boys put away their fiddles, she told me she had never had such a good time.

"Then marry me," I said.

"Don't spoil this," she said. "I feel like Cinderella after the ball. And you know I ain't the marrying kind. Geese mate for life, not people."

I didn't mention it again.

"Kid," Doolin said, walking over and tugging on the brim of his hat for Lucinda. "We have work today. Do you think it would be all right if your dance partner rode back in with Edith and some of the other ladies in the wagon?"

I looked questioningly at her.

"With Edith there," she said, "I think I can handle anything."

Lucinda stood on her toes and kissed me on the cheek.

Eleven

It was one of those bright, not-too-cold days that almost makes winter seem tolerable. Doolin, Bitter Creek, and I made a leisurely ride north to Red Rock, about twenty-five miles to the northwest, in Noble County.

Doolin drew to a halt in front of the green railroad depot.

"We're going to hit the Santa Fe?" Bitter Creek asked.

"It would be a good day for it, according to Bill Dalton's intelligence," Doolin said. "There's supposed to be a big payroll coming down."

"It could be a trap," Bitter Creek said.

"That's what I aim to find out," Doolin said. "One of us is going to ride on that train from Red Rock to Perry to check it out. Kid, how well do you trust your brother?"

"Well enough," I said. "You want me to do it?"

"I would be obliged."

I dismounted and handed the reins to Doolin. Then I unbuckled my gun belt and hung it from Cimarron's saddle horn.

"Don't you want to hang on to your gun?" Bitter Creek asked.

"Not if it's a trap," I said. "It would just give them an excuse to fill me full of lead, and I'm not foolish enough to think I can outshoot a whole trainload of U.S. marshals. Besides, the damn conductor is likely to take a dim view of me hoofing up and down the aisles with iron on my hip."

"Have enough money for the ticket?" Doolin asked.

I said I did.

"Adios," Doolin said. "Get off at Perry—if you can."

Doolin and Bitter Creek rode off toward the south, leading Cimarron, who was bogging down because it felt unnatural to leave me behind. Feeling unusually light, I walked into the depot to buy my ticket. The clerk didn't give me a second look, even when I asked him if the train was on schedule. He said it was. There was about an hour to kill, so I sat outside on one of the benches facing the tracks.

I pulled my hat low over my eyes and tried to nap.

"Beautiful day, ain't it?"

I grunted and peeked out from beneath the brim. A man in a rumpled brown suit sat down beside me. He wore a bowler hat and under his arm was a newspaper. He put his hands in his pockets and his jacket slipped back enough that I could see the star pinned on his vest.

"It's the kind of day that makes you feel glad to be alive," the man went on. "You know, I read stories in the papers"—he tapped the *Kansas City Star* under his arm—"about folks who do themselves in for one reason or another, usually for love, but I just can't understand it. What could be so bad to make you want to kill yourself, eh? Well, I guess any fool can eat a box of match heads when the going becomes difficult."

I couldn't help myself.

"Match heads?" I asked.

"Yes, it's right here," he said, thumping the paper. "Match heads—they're poisonous, you know. A young fellow involved in an unfortunate love triangle ate a whole box of them in Olathe the day before yesterday. Killed him deader than a doornail."

"Shame," I said from beneath my hat.

"Not really," the man said, and sniffed. "An individual like that is just not a valuable member of society. The rest of us are better off without him. Take the Daltons, for instance."

"Oh?" I asked.

"Yes," he said. "The good citizens of Coffeyville did the rest of us a favor when they blew the Dalton boys to hell. What fools—to think they could rob two banks at the same time. Of course, I was headed to Coffeyville to help defend the town, but I got there an hour too late. I had been trailing the Daltons for months, you know."

"You don't say."

"Why, yes. Oh, I'm sorry—I haven't introduced myself. I am Special Agent Ransom Payne. The railroads hired me." He held out his hand. "And who might you be?"

I slid my hat back and shook his hand.

"Call me Dick," I said. "Dick Turpin."

There was no glimmer of recognition in his eyes. The man looked like an alcoholic walrus, with his red bulbous nose and his mop of whiskers below.

"I guess you're out of a job since the Dalton gang was shot to pieces," I ventured.

"Oh no," he said. "Not all of the gang were killed. There are still some desperadoes on the loose, and it is those individuals I'm tracking now. There

was a sixth bandit escaped from Coffeyville—
eyewitnesses reported seeing six riders come into
town, but when the shooting stopped, there were
only five outlaws accounted for—and this sixth man
and some other Dalton alumni are apparently part
of a new gang called the Wild Bunch."

"No," I said. "Do you have a description of
this sixth rider?"

Payne made a sour face.

"Well, the reports differ. Some say he was Bill
Doolin, a former cowboy who sometimes rode with
the Daltons. The story is that his horse went lame
and he had to turn back at the last minute. But the
eyewitness descriptions don't match Doolin, who is
tall and redheaded. According to T. C. Babb, the
cashier in the Condon Bank, the sixth man had long
sandy-colored hair and was of medium height. He
wore a buckskin shirt, something like yours, and
rode a blood bay."

"Imagine that," I said. "Say, what're you doing
on the Sante Fe? Am I going to see some action
today—do you have a trap set for the Wild Bunch?"

Payne laughed.

"Nothing of the sort. I'm headed down to the
Creek Nation, where I understand the new gang has
some sort of cave fortress. You might say I'm recon-
noitering the area."

"So you're going to make your report to the
Pinkertons before assaulting this outlaw fortress?"

"No, I don't work for the Pinkertons," he said,
and sniffed. "I am a special agent employed directly
by the railway. I answer only to myself and, of
course, the president."

"Of the United States?"

"No, the railroad. Hell and damnation, you
cowboys don't know much, do you?"

Eventually the train came huffing and clanging

into the station. I followed Payne into the first car and took a seat beside him so I could keep an eye on the great detective. He loved to talk, as long as the subject was himself, and inside of half an hour I felt that my ears had been chewed down to stubs.

I excused myself and walked all the way to the express car and back, and saw nothing out of the ordinary. There weren't many passengers and the train appeared to have only the usual number of crew—engineer, fireman, brakeman, conductor. I didn't have access to the express car, of course, but I listened at the door and heard nothing to make me suspect it was loaded with marshals. If it had been, they surely would have been chatting and joking among themselves.

If there was a payroll on that train, it was ripe for the picking.

When I returned to my seat, I found that Payne had mercifully gone to sleep beneath his bowler. We were just a few miles from Perry. I thought about taking his gun and forcing him off the train, to hold him for ransom at the Rock Fort, or to otherwise let him know that I was a Dalton and that he was the fool, but it was just too risky. He had spent too much time with me, and even if he was a braggart and a coward, he could identify me.

So I tied the laces of his shoes together.

Twelve

We caught the mail hack going north out of Ingalls on March 15, 1893. It was Edith's twentieth birthday and Doolin allowed how it would be the perfect day for their marriage. Their choice of location was even more significant, considering that Edith was about to marry into the outlaw life—at my brother Bill's invitation, the ceremony was held at the home of our mother, Adelaine Younger Dalton. Maybe, I thought, Ma could give Edith some tips on how to cope with the uncertainty and constant fear of death that came with loving outlaws. Edith knew the truth about Doolin, of course; there was nobody in Ingalls who *didn't*. You can't traipse around with Winchesters, spending lots of money and being wary of strangers, without being pegged for an outlaw. I even think that Edith was kind of proud of Doolin for being known as the "King of the Oklahoma Outlaws," just in the same way that a banker's wife or a railway president is proud of her husband.

Doolin at least *looked* like a bank president, in his dark hat and suit, with a flower in the lapel. Bitter Creek was dressed like the rake he was, in a fancy striped suit with brocaded vest. I had temporarily traded in my buckskin shirt and jeans for dark pants and an old-fashioned frock coat, but I kept my black hat with the beaded band. All of us were heavy with revolvers. Mine was riding on my hip beneath my coat, and I had a .32-caliber backup tucked into my right boot. Except for the guns, folks might have mistaken us for three successful merchants on a business trip. There weren't any creases in our pants, either, so there was no way that folks could mistake our clothes for the cheap store-bought kind.

Edith wore the white dress she was going to be married in, and she was careful of the mud getting in and out of the mail coach. Lucinda wore a plain gingham dress, but it didn't seem to make her look any plainer—no matter what she wore, it always seemed like she was about to bust out of it.

Doolin was in a rare fine mood, full of smiles and easy talk, and when the five of us changed over to the Rock Island for the short hop over to Kingfisher, he chatted with the conductor like he was an old friend. The rest of us were in good spirits as well; all, that is, except Bitter Creek, who took to glumly staring out the window. It was my guess that he was thinking about Rose Dunn.

We arrived in Kingfisher early that afternoon. There was quite a bit of activity at the depot, people bustling here and there with packages and important-looking papers and luggage, and as we made our way through it, no one made eye contact with us. There we were, the chief and two lieutenants of the most notorious robber gang since the Jameses, and we were taking a stroll in broad daylight through a couple of hundred people without being noticed. Doolin said it was because folks

didn't expect to find us there, at least not in city
duds, accompanied by two women, and getting *off*
a train instead of boarding one.

"Watch this," Doolin said.

A U.S. deputy marshal was leaning against a
post, his thumbs hooked in his belt, looking bored.
Doolin stuck a cigar in the corner of his mouth and
asked the marshal for a light. With exaggerated
slowness the marshal pulled a match from his shirt
pocket, struck it on the post, and cupped the flame
between his two rough hands.

Doolin bent over—giving the marshal a good
look at his face—stuck the end of the cigar into the
flame, and sucked fire into it.

"Thanks," Doolin said.

"*De nada,*" returned the marshal, whipping out
the match.

"Say," Doolin said, gesturing with the cigar,
"you wouldn't know where we might find the Methodist church, would you?"

"Sure," the marshal said, and he pushed away
from the post. "Go down this street four blocks,
then take a right, and it's three blocks west. Brand-
new church, you can't miss it."

"Obliged," Doolin said, and touched a finger to
the brim of his hat.

"Did you hear?" Doolin asked when he came
back to us.

"We heard," Bitter Creek said. "We'll see you
at the house."

"Give it about two hours," Doolin said.

Bitter Creek and I found a saloon and drank whiskey until the middle of the afternoon. I reckon we
might have passed the time a little too well, because
when I stood up the saloon spun around me and I

had to grab hold of Bitter Creek's shoulder to keep from falling. But Bitter Creek was not in much better shape, and he staggered under my weight and we both fell in a heap. Bitter Creek's .45 fell out of his shoulder holster onto the floor.

Then we started laughing and couldn't stop.

The bartender looked unhappily at us but was afraid to say anything. Bitter Creek picked up the gun, slipped it back inside his shoulder holster, and used a chair to pull himself up. Then he extended a hand and pulled me to my feet. Still laughing, we brushed each other off.

"There's a city ordinance against carrying concealed weapons," said a soft-spoken man standing at the bar. "Not to mention," he added, "public drunkenness."

"We ain't drunk, mister," Bitter Creek said, grinning.

"You could have fooled me," the man at the bar said. He had his right boot wedged under the brass rail, but he turned enough for us to see his face—and the badge upon his chest.

"Sorry, Constable," I said, trying unsuccessfully to clear my head. "We came out here for a friend's wedding and I guess we've just had too much of a good time. We won't be no trouble, honest."

"I know you won't," he said. "Because you and your friend are going to give me those guns."

I saw the look in Bitter Creek's eyes—he was ready to kill somebody. I had to think quick, and the world was still tilted pretty badly. If I let Bitter Creek kill this city constable, it might put a damper on Doolin's wedding. I tried hard to think what my brother Bob might have done. *So what do you do with a lawman if you can't kill him?* I seemed to hear him say. *Hell, you buy him off.*

"Look here, Captain," I said. "My friend here

was just ignorant of your laws. From now on, he'll keep his pistol in his belt, where you can see it. Won't you, Bit—Biddlebaum."

Christ, I had almost called him Bitter Creek.

I took the .45 from Bitter Creek's shoulder holster and tucked it into his belt.

"And seeing as how you caught us dead to rights the first time, I reckon there's a fine to pay," I said. As I walked over to the constable I took a wad of money from my pants pocket and picked out two ten-dollar bills. I tucked the twenty dollars into his shirt pocket. "Can we just call it even, hoss?"

The constable looked uncomfortable, but nodded.

"Fine," I said. "Biddlebaum and I will be going now. They're holding a wedding for us, you know. No more trouble from us, I swear."

We left the saloon and went in search of a minister.

"Biddlebaum?" Bitter Creek asked.

We were still more than a little drunk and it seemed like it took us forever to find the Methodist church. When we did find it, it was kind of a disappointment; it was a tiny, unpainted affair and it didn't even have a bell tower. It did, however, have a sign out front that said that services were at ten A.M. on Sundays, and that the minister was the Reverend Frederick Phister. We found the good reverend in his shoebox-sized office inside the church. He had his coat off and was eating a ham sandwich over his desk while trying to write his sermon for Sunday.

"Could I help you gentlemen?" he asked suspiciously as Bitter Creek and I crowded in the door. There wasn't room for us inside the office.

Phister wore glasses that looked like they came from the bottoms of a couple of beer bottles and he had a bald head the light shone from. He sat there with an expectant look on his face, a napkin tucked into his shirt, the sandwich poised in his left hand, a fountain pen in his right. He took another bite of the sandwich and his Adam's apple bobbed above his open collar.

"Excuse us, Reverend," Bitter Creek said in the voice he saved for flirting with women and conversing with fools. "Hate to disturb you like this, but we have a little problem that I believe you can help us with."

"Yes?" Phister asked.

"You're needed at a wedding."

"I beg your pardon?"

"You have some marryin' to do," Bitter Creek said.

Phister shook his head.

"You must be mistaken," he said. He had laid down the sandwich and the pen and was shuffling through the papers on his desk as if he'd forgotten something. "I have no weddings to perform today."

"You do now," Bitter Creek said, and pulled his coat back far enough to reveal the butt of his revolver.

"Don't worry," I said. "You'll be coming back, as long as you promise to keep your mouth shut. We hate to do this to you, Reverend, but in our line of work it just ain't convenient to schedule things in advance."

Phister screwed up his courage and asked, "What kind of work are you in?"

"Oh," I said. "Haven't you guessed? We're outlaws."

Phister went white.

"Come on," Bitter Creek said. "Get your coat. This won't take long, and we ain't gonna hurt you—as long as you do your part. We'd hate for anything about our boss's wedding to go wrong.

Now, you don't have anything from me to worry about, but my partner here doesn't like preachers."

"You don't?" Phister asked me.

"Sort of made a speciality of shooting preachers back where I come from," I said. "It was a bad habit—there was too many of 'em, they were much too slow, and they was mostly unarmed—so I determined to give it up. But I have a bad spell now and then that ends in a relapse."

"He's joking, right?" Phister asked Bitter Creek.

"Don't you have a book or something you read out of?"

"Oh, yes," he said, and took a slim volume from the desk.

"Need anything else?" I asked.

He shook his head.

"Think we ought to blindfold him?" Bitter Creek asked.

"Naw," I said. "I think we can trust him. Can we trust you, Reverend?"

"Oh, yes," he said, nodding his head vigorously.

"Don't worry," Bitter Creek said. "The Kid here hasn't potted a preacher in a month of Sundays. Of course, that could mean he's due."

We were an hour late and Doolin was beginning to fret by the time we arrived at my mother's house. He came out the front door of the little white frame house and met us in the yard.

"Where have you boys been? How difficult could it be to find a preacher and ask him to come back here with—" Doolin waved a hand in front of his face. "Phew. Both of you are crocked, ain't you? Jesus! Sorry, Reverend."

Phister smiled sweetly and Bitter Creek shrugged.

Doolin looked closer at both of us.

"You didn't abuse the reverend, did you?"

"Well—" I began.

"They didn't pull guns on you, did they, sir?"

"Actually, we did—"

"Jesus," Doolin said again. "You *kidnapped* the preacher for my wedding? You went into his church and forced him to come with you *at gunpoint*?"

"Well—" I tried again.

Doolin held his head in his hands.

"Don't tell me," he said. "I can't get married this way. Reverend, I apologize for the way the boys have treated you. You're free to go."

Phister straightened his jacket and looked smugly at Bitter Creek and me.

"I have a good mind to report you to the law," Phister said.

"I wouldn't blame you a bit," Doolin said.

Phister turned to go.

"Oh, Reverend," Doolin said. "I'd like to make a small donation to your church. I know it won't make up for all the trouble the boys have been"— Doolin pressed thirty dollars into his hand—"but I hope you'll accept this with Bill Doolin's compliments. Perhaps you'd like to stay and perform the service after all? Of course, I am prepared to compensate you for whatever you feel your time is worth."

Phister was hooked. He slipped the notes into his pocket and allowed that since he was already there, it made no sense to go back to town—as long as there were no more misunderstandings.

"We would expect you to be discreet," Doolin said.

"Of course," Phister replied.

Doolin walked him inside the house.

"Well," Bitter Creek said, and slapped me on the shoulder, "it seems we were using the wrong bait all along. We should have appealed to his Christian duty—and crossed his palm with thirty pieces of silver."

I laughed until I saw my mother standing in the doorway.

My brother Bill had been true to his word to keep silent, and under the best of circumstances it would have been difficult explaining my presence to Ma, but I had pretty much made the worst out of the situation—I had whiskey on my breath, I had hijacked a preacher at gunpoint, and the girl I was regularly committing mortal sin with was sitting in the parlor.

"Howdy, Ma," I said.

It was not the right thing to say, but then I don't know if there would have been a right thing. Bitter Creek slipped on inside the house and left us to settle it in the yard. Ma was really sore at me for not letting her know I was alive, but I told her that I was trying to protect her so that U.S. marshals wouldn't be constantly hounding her. She said that was no excuse. I told her that she would feel differently when detectives started throwing bombs in the house—which, I pointed out, is precisely what happened to the poor mother of Jesse and Frank James. Then Ma started crying, which put a damper on my argument, and I finally admitted that she was right and asked her to forgive me, which she eventually did.

Then she asked me about Lucinda, and I told a whopper about us being engaged to be married, and how she clerked in the same store that Edith worked in, and what a regular churchgoer she was. Ma said that she looked like a sweet girl and that I had better give up the outlaw trail like Doolin and prepare to settle down and raise some kids.

"Doolin said he was quitting?" I asked.

"Yes, he did," Ma said.

I didn't mind lying to my ma, but it riled me that Doolin was at it, too.

"And, Samuel," she said, "you'd better give up drinking as well. You know what it did to your father, and your brothers."

"Honestly, Ma," I said. "Grat didn't live long enough for it to be a problem, and neither did Frank. And maybe Bob's problem was that he didn't drink enough—if he'd been nursing a bottle of whiskey instead of his pride, maybe he wouldn't have tried two banks at once."

My mother gave me a look that threatened to break my heart.

"Sorry, Ma," I said.

"You boys are killing me, do you know that?" she asked. "What happened to you younger boys? What was it that filled your heads with such foolishness?"

"I don't know, Ma."

Then we went inside for the wedding.

Phister hitched Edith and Doolin together real proper, with lots of talk about love, honor, and obedience. Edith was happy, but Doolin was in a peculiar mood. Oh, he was smiling, all right, and acting like it was the biggest day of his life, but he seemed a little daunsy around the edges. No matter how much happiness they managed to steal in one day, Doolin knew what lay ahead for them, and it was going to be a damn sight harder on Edith than on him.

When the happy couple had left on their honeymoon—they were going to spend a week living the high life in hotels in Kingfisher and Guthrie—my brother Bill came up to me and shook my hand.

"What's that for?" I asked.

"You just look so damn respectable in those duds," he said. "Get your hair trimmed up and you would pass in any circle."

"Nope," I said. "Nobody cuts my hair."

"Like Samson that way?" Bill asked.

"No," I said. "But I ought to be more like Midas, to keep up this kind of life. It's downright expensive."

"Seems you've picked up all sorts of bad habits," Bill said, looking at Lucinda. "Ma asked her about church, you know, and she said it wasn't necessary for her to go—that all the preachers come to her." He turned back to me. "Whew! Your breath is like a distillery. Sam, you didn't used to drink."

"Spare me the lectures," I said. "What have you heard about Emmett?"

"You don't know?" Bill asked. "Guess you haven't kept up with the newspapers. Emmett pleaded guilty to the killings of Cubine and Brown, just like he was supposed to, and Judge McCue promptly sentenced him to life in prison."

Thirteen

With Emmett serving a life sentence at the Kansas Penitentiary at Lansing, the escape plans were back on. Problem was, I had been dipping into my creekside "bank" a little too often for Lucinda and myself—you'd be amazed at what whiskey and fine clothes and baubles cost— and the war chest for Em's escape was getting slim. I was relieved when Doolin announced another big job—the biggest, in fact, so far.

We were going to hit the Santa Fe's Southern California and New Mexico express just outside Cimarron, Kansas. The men that Doolin picked for the job included Bitter Creek, as second in command; Bill Dalton, because the job was based on his information and it could be the gang's "big casino"; myself, as all-purpose ramrod; and two new members of the gang—Tulsa Jack Blake and Dynamite Dick Clifton.

Tulsa Jack was a reckless Kansas cowboy who had lost his job a few years back and drifted into the Oklahoma Territory. He was a big, brooding man with a flowing black mustache. He was reputed to be a dead shot and had gotten his nickname from spending too much time playing faro at Tulsa. In many ways he reminded me of my brother Grat.

Dynamite Dick was a small-sized fellow with fair hair and no beard who made up in shrewdness what he might have lacked in strength. He had been a cattle rustler and a whiskey peddler in the Chickasaw Nation before graduating to the Wild Bunch. His nickname came from his nasty habit of hollowing out the lead tips of his bullets and filling them with dynamite so they exploded on impact.

I spent the night before we headed out with Lucinda in her tiny room at Sadie Comley's. We had come to an uneasy truce over her whoring: she slacked off some but kept it up, and I pretended not to notice. Neither of us talked much about it anymore. Lord knows she didn't need to do it to support herself any longer, because I was giving her plenty of money.

After we had made love, and she was lying in my arms real peaceful, I told her I was going to leave her three hundred dollars, which was the last of the money I had hidden away from the earlier jobs.

"I'm afraid that I'll get killed and you wouldn't know where to find it," I said.

"Keep your money," she said. "You'll be back."

"No, listen," I said. "I want you to get your teeth fixed. I'm sure there's a dentist somewhere who can fix them up fine. You deserve it. I just wanted you to have it now in case . . ."

I was too superstitious to finish the sentence.

"Thanks," she said.

Lucinda began to cry. The tears dropped from her cheeks onto my arm.

"What's wrong?" I asked.

"Nobody's ever done anything that nice for

me," she said, and sniffed. "I'm not used to it. And I'm angry with you, too. Damn you, Sam Dalton, I think I'm falling in love with you. What am I going to do if you get yourself killed?"

"It won't happen," I said.

She laughed.

"Don't bullshit me," she said. "We both know it's going to happen. It's just a matter of time. I'm sorry if I've violated one of your taboos having to do with talking about it, but those are the facts. And you know what I feel really bad about? Every time we've been together, the knowledge that you might not make it back from the next job made our love-making just that much more exciting. Lord, how's that for wickedness?"

"I understand," I said. "I have to confess your whoring didn't make me want you any less. I mean, I've wanted you to stop and all, but in bed . . . Well, it just made me want you more. And I reckon that's pretty damn wicked as well."

Lucky sighed.

"Damn you," she said. "I can't be in love with you, Sam Dalton, I just can't. It complicates everything. I'm going to start worrying about who you're with, and what you're doing, and when you're gonna be back. Damn you for being so good to me. Why can't you treat me shitty like all the other men in my life have done? Beat me up some before you poke me."

"You don't mean that."

She damned me again. Then she sighed and buried her head against my chest. I still loved how clean and good she smelled, and how she felt when she was against me.

"What're we gonna do with our wicked selves?" she asked.

• • •

I slipped out of Lucinda's window an hour before dawn while she still slept. It's easier than it sounds, because it probably would have taken an explosion to get her up. Anyway, I didn't want to have to say good-bye.

It was spring and the morning air smelled fresh and good. I walked to the livery and found the boy, Del Simmons, sitting by a kerosene lamp waiting for me. Cimarron was saddled and ready to go. The horse was well-groomed and the saddle had been soaped and oiled. My bedroll and rain slicker were rolled tight and tied behind the saddle.

"You going to hit a bank or a train this time?" he asked as I slid the Winchester into its scabbard.

The question surprised me.

"How do you know what we're up to?" I asked.

"Oh, that's easy," he said. "The whole gang is taking their finest horses this morning. Fast horses, too—racehorses. And you're all armed like you're ready to start a war. Besides, people have been talking about it in town all week, how Doolin has decided it was time to pull another job. The only thing folks don't know is what you're going to hit."

"Can't tell you," I said. "But I guarantee you'll read about it in the papers in a few days. How's Cimarron?"

"He's fine," Del said. "His coat looks real healthy, don't it? I've been giving him cod liver oil."

Doolin and Bitter Creek rode up outside. Their horses had been at the other livery.

"You ready?" Doolin asked.

"Almost," I said. I swung up into the saddle.

"You've done a fine job," I told the kid. I dug in my shirt pocket and handed down a ten-dollar note. It was probably more money in one place than the kid had seen in his life, but then I was in the habit of overpaying folks.

"Thanks," he said. "I'll be watching the papers."

"If I don't come back," I asked, "can you do something for me?"

"Anything."

"Tell Lucky to get her teeth fixed."

For the next few days we followed the Cimarron River northwest into Kansas, then turned and made directly for Gray County, which is just west of Dodge City. About dark on the afternoon of Thursday, June 9, we pulled up to a farm about four miles north of Cimarron town.

We were surprised to find an old-fashioned, swaybacked prairie schooner being loaded by the family who lived there. Every possession they owned seemed to be crammed inside or tied somehow to the outside.

"Good Lord," Doolin said from atop his horse. "What's going on here?"

"We're busted," the man said. He was balding, with a crown of thick dark hair over his ears, and he wore a work shirt that was stained almost black with dirt and sweat. "Between the bankers and the weather, we're finished. We are going back east, where my parents came from fifty years ago in this wagon. I reckon that's where they ought to have stayed."

Two little girls cowered behind his legs as he spoke to us, and the man's sorry wife looked on from the doorway of their ramshackle home. The son, who appeared to be about fourteen, kept up with his work and pretended our presence didn't bother him. There was a ten-gauge shotgun leaning against the wagon, within arm's reach of the father.

"Mister, we're mighty sorry to hear about your bad luck," Doolin said. "We don't want to trouble you folks, but we were looking for someplace to bed down for the night. Maybe some feed for our horses. We'd pay, of course."

"We weren't going to leave until morning anyway," the man said. "There's grain in the barn. Help yourselves."

"Peter," the woman said sternly. "We don't know anything about these men."

"Oh, hell," the man fumed. "There's six of them, and each of them has a pair of Colts and a Winchester, at the least. If they want to rob us, they're going to do it no matter what we say—at least it would be a damn sight more honest than how the banks robbed us, telling us how we could afford two mortgages on this place."

"We ain't gonna rob you," Doolin said quietly. "I'm Bill Doolin and this here is the Wild Bunch. That's Bitter Creek Newcomb, and this is Bill Dalton. The Choctaw Kid is there. You wouldn't have heard yet of the other two, because they're new."

The wife damn near fainted, but the husband took it in stride.

"Pleased to meet you," he said, scratching his chin whiskers. "I'm Peter Potter. You gonna rob a bank or a train this time out?"

"A train," Doolin said.

"Good. The bastards helped put me out of business. An honest man just can't make a living anymore, squeezed as he is between the banks and the railroads."

Potter invited us to take supper with the family, and when the wife finally saw we weren't going to scalp or murder them, she became a little warmer as well. The meal wasn't much, just beans and corn bread and coffee, and some milk for the little girls, but it was enough. There wasn't any furniture left in the house, so we all ate on the floor, with our plates in our laps.

"Lots of folks are going back," Potter said over dinner. "Last year, do you know there were eighteen thousand wagons crossed the Missouri River, going back east? It's a fact. All fifty-year-old wrecks like the one out front—can you imagine? I hate to leave. My folks is buried out there under that tree, you know. But what choice do we have? The mortgage payments on this place are killing us, and there hasn't been a decent crop in five years. What profit there has been in wheat, the railroads have gouged out of us. I'm not against your kind at all, no sir. In my mind, you're performing a public service."

Doolin nodded.

"What d'you call your little girls?"

You could see the man soften as he talked about his children.

"That's Lola and Ellie," he said. "Twins. Aren't they something? And the big boy is Pete Junior—he acts a little peculiar around strangers, but I'm real proud of him. There's another boy, John, buried out back with my folks. The fever got him three years ago."

"How much would it take?" Doolin asked. "To stay, I mean."

"Three hundred dollars," the man said. "Catch up the mortgage and make sure we had seed for the next crop. But if I could have gotten that kind of money, I would have stayed. Besides, there's no guarantee there'll be a crop this year or next. It could be just throwing good money after bad."

"But you hate to leave," Doolin said.

"I hate to fail," Potter said. "You know how it

is, with a family depending upon you. The boy and I could shift for ourselves, but I hate to let the wife and these little girls down. But this state is going to hell in a handbasket, anyway. Woman suffrage will carry in Kansas, and it will make the state Republican for years to come."

"How do you figure that?" Doolin asked.

"Most females don't necessarily vote as their husbands do, but Republican women will because of the power of the state organizations—it's something like a denominational issue. Then you have your cities and towns, where the women are largely under the influence of preachers. The women can't have a meeting unless they can find a preacher to run it, and the preachers are ninety-percent Republican. So there you have it."

Doolin nodded.

"Goddamned Republicans are ruining this country for everybody except the banks and the railroads," Potter said.

"I agree," Doolin said.

"At least you're doing something about it," Potter said wistfully.

"So are you," Doolin said. "You're feeding us, ain't you?"

"Yes," Potter said, and he seemed to grow a couple of inches taller. "I guess we are extending aid and comfort to the sworn enemies of banks and railroads everywhere."

"Damn right," Doolin said. Then, to the wife: "Sorry."

"You young folks better remember this meal," Potter said. "This will be something to tell your own kids about, that during our last night on our own spread in Kansas, we fed Bill Doolin and his Wild Bunch."

"This meal was mighty good, ma'am," Doolin

said, brushing his mustache. He removed his hat, tossed in a handful of greenbacks, and passed it among the boys. "I suggest you throw in what you got," he told us, "because tomorrow you either will have plenty more, or won't be needing what you got."

When the hat came back to Doolin he turned it over, dumping its contents on the floor in front of the couple. A gold piece rolled a foot or so away from the pile of notes and made that peculiar circle that coins sometimes do as they come to a stop. I don't know how much was there, because we didn't count it, but judging from the size of the pile, there had to be at least a hundred.

"Much obliged for the meal," Doolin said. "This ain't enough to save your place, but maybe it will make the trip back a mite smoother. And we'd be obliged if you wouldn't mention us to anybody along the way."

At dawn the Potters hitched eight mules to their ancient Conestoga and pulled out for the East. We stayed for most of the day at the deserted farm, letting the horses rest up. At sundown we mounted up and rode toward Cimarron, and stopped a half mile west of town, at a bridge on the Santa Fe's transcontinental line to California.

The bridge spanned the Arkansas River, and for crossing such a shallow body of water, it was a regular monument. We tied the horses underneath the bridge and settled in.

Doolin said we had about five hours to kill.

Fourteen

Waiting is the hardest part of most any job. Imagination can get the best of you before a single cap is busted, and you can suffer through a dozen different but equally horrible deaths in your mind. You can get yourself so spooked that when it's time to go to work, you have yourself convinced that you're going to die—and when that happens, you're no good to anybody, least of all yourself, and somebody *is* likely to get killed.

Each member of the Wild Bunch had their own way of passing the time, and it involved whatever sin they had a particular weakness for: women, cards, or whiskey. Bitter Creek could usually find a willing female, and my brother Bill fancied himself as something of a gambler despite the money he lost. From the little I knew about them, since they were so new to the gang, Tulsa Jack and Dynamite Dan were drinkers. What did I do? Well, I read—Blake or Coleridge or Defoe, if I could get them, or just about anything if I couldn't. The main thing was to shut down that voice in my head, to drown it out with somebody else's voice, to simply not allow myself to think about my brothers and Coffeyville and all the things that could go wrong.

Doolin was the only one who managed to stay levelheaded without resorting to some kind of trick, and I think it was just part of his natural leadership ability. Doolin couldn't read or write, other than his name, but he knew how to command an outlaw gang, and much of what he did was done by example.

That night, waiting beneath the bridge, Doolin sat on the ground with his Winchester across his knees, as cool and collected as if he were sitting on his own front porch. He did have his own front porch in Ingalls now, since his marriage to Edith Ellsworth; they lived in a little white house that was between Wagoner's blacksmith shop and the O.K. Hotel.

The problem with the rest of us was that it was impossible to do anything beneath that cursed bridge for the five hours we had to wait since sundown. There were no women, of course, and the nearest real saloon was across the line in Oklahoma Territory, since Kansas was dry. Doolin hadn't allowed Tulsa Jack or Dynamite Dan to even carry a bottle in their saddlebags. It was too dark to play cards or to read, and making any kind of light beneath the bridge was out of the question.

So we sat and waited and took turns pulling watch on the bridge. I liked watch best because it wasn't as suffocating as sitting in the blackness beneath the bridge with five others. So I grabbed my rifle and climbed on top. I sat on the trestle, and each way for as far as the eye could see, the rails were clear. Far off to the east, you could just make out the lights of the depot at Cimarron.

It was a warm night and the sky was clear.

There were more stars than I ever remembered seeing before, and the Milky Way stretched across
the sky like a starry smudge. I wondered if, across
the vast oceans of ether, there were people on those
stars, like Professor Lowell says. While I am looking
at the stars I am always sure there *are* people up
there, but I don't know if the thought frightens or
comforts me. Thinking about other worlds got me
to thinking about God, and thinking about God got
me to thinking about people's souls, and whether
you know anything after you're dead. Then I realized I had done it to myself again, that I was thinking morbid thoughts, and I wished it were light
enough to read. I determined to start memorizing
poems and such so that I could recite them to myself
and not need a book in front of me.

In an hour I came down from the bridge, having seen nothing but a couple of coyotes cross the
rails like ghosts, and Bitter Creek went up to stand
the last watch. Doolin was still sitting on the
ground, with his hat pulled low over his eyes. Next
to him was my brother Bill, fiddling with his guns
for the thousandth time. Tulsa Jack and Dynamite
had their backs against a couple of pilings.

"Kid," Doolin said, "what time's your watch
say?"

I took out my pocket watch.

"Midnight," I said. "Straight up."

"I do hope the train is on time," Doolin said.
"Let's go."

My brother Bill, Tulsa Jack, and Dynamite
would stay at the bridge. Doolin, Bitter Creek, and
I started walking down the tracks toward Cimarron.

Ten minutes later we were at the Santa Fe depot. After making sure the depot was deserted except for the agent, we walked inside. Doolin had his
hat pulled down low over his eyes and his kerchief

bunched up in front, leaving little of his face showing. Bitter Creek and I hung back and hid our rifles beneath our dusters.

The agent was an old fellow with gray chin whiskers and thick glasses. He looked like he was about ready to fall asleep before we walked in.

Doolin and the agent exchanged nods.

"Is the Express on time?" Doolin inquired. He was looking down at the floor and most of what the agent could see was Doolin's black Stetson.

The agent rubbed his eyes and consulted his messages for the night. "No," he said. "It ain't. She's exactly an hour late. Be through at one-ten, but, mister, it don't stop here."

Doolin hesitated. I knew he was weighing the advantages of staying versus coming back later. The agent surely would be suspicious of anybody asking questions about the Express at this hour, and if we came back we could get a nasty surprise.

"Mister," the agent repeated, "I said it doesn't stop."

"Tonight she does," Doolin said.

"Oh?" the agent asked indignantly. "Who says?"

"We do," Doolin said.

Bitter Creek and I uncovered our Winchesters and pointed them at about the spot where the man buttoned his collar. His attitude improved at once. We already had our kerchiefs over our noses.

"You fellows are right as rain," he said. "It does stop."

"Shut up and keep your hands up where we can see 'em," Doolin said as he pulled his kerchief up. He leaned over and rummaged in the agent's desk for the gun he knew was there. He finally found it, an old Schofield with a heavy coat of rust. He dropped the gun in the water tank by the door.

"Now, we want you to give the message to hold the train for orders," Doolin said, "so go outside and hoist that red ball or whatever it is you do. And you had better do it right, because you're the first one we'll kill if the train crew is in the least suspicious."

The agent nodded.

"What are you waiting for?" Bitter Creek asked. "Move!"

"Yes, sir. But I can do it from here," the agent said.

"You don't have to go outside?"

"No, sir. This series of levers are connected to the semaphore."

"Do it," Doolin said. "But just do it right. And be sure to keep your hands away from the telegraphic key, unless you'd like to lose some fingers."

When the agent had finished setting the semaphore, Bitter Creek and I tied him up with some rope we brought with us, gagged him with a handkerchief, and eased him to the floor of his office, where he couldn't be seen by the passing train crew.

"Don't worry," Doolin told him. "This is just to keep you out of trouble."

"Another hour?" Bitter Creek asked. "What do we do now?"

"Well," Doolin said, "you get back down the track and tell the rest of the boys that the Express is late, then come on back. The Kid and I will stay here and hope nobody comes by or tries to raise the old man on the telegraph. Say, do you know Morse?"

"Nope," Bitter Creek said.

"How about you?" he asked me.

"Not a letter of it," I said.

"Damn. It would be a good thing to study on," Doolin suggested.

Bitter Creek left.

"Do you think we ought to douse the lights?" Doolin asked.

"No," I said. "The depot is open all night. If you kill the lights, folks might take more notice than if you left them burning."

Doolin nodded. He pulled one of the benches around and placed it near the end of the counter so he had a good view of the front door and the agent. I took up a position on the other side of the room. As luck would have it, someone had left a copy of the *Cimarron New West* on the bench.

The Express turned out to be an hour and ten minutes late. At 1:20 A.M. the floor of the depot began to shake, and from the platform you could see the big headlight advancing double fast. The engine screamed past the depot like a shot, belching smoke and embers as it went.

"It didn't stop," I shouted over the noise.

"It will," Doolin said. "They were just high-balling it and not prepared to stop. Can you hear that metallic squeal? They're applying the brakes right now."

Doolin was right. The procession of cars began to slow.

"You and Bitter Creek start on up toward the engine," Doolin said. "I'll stay here and give the conductor his orders when he comes. Wait for my signal before moving out."

I ducked beneath one of the couplings between the passenger cars and came out on the far side of the train. Bitter Creek and I reached the engine at about the same time, pulled up our masks, and clambered up on either side of the cab.

"What the hell is this?" the engineer roared.

"An unscheduled stop," Bitter Creek said.

He threw his Winchester to his shoulder and aimed at the man's head. I covered the fireman. He didn't seem the type for heroics, but you never knew. Engineers, on the other hand, were always trouble—they were too used to having their own way.

"Who the hell are you?" the engineer asked.

"Oh, I'll bet you could guess," Bitter Creek said. "Now shut up for a minute, won't you?"

Bitter Creek's gun barrel wavered as he glanced back toward the depot, and the engineer's sharp eyes followed it. He seemed about ready to spring and take the rifle away from Bitter Creek. I pointed my rifle over at the engineer and shook my head.

"There's the signal," Bitter Creek said. "Okay, hoss, let's move this train out nice and slow. I want you to take us to the whistle-stop, a half mile west of town, just before the bridge. Understand?"

"Sure," the engineer said.

The engineer eased the throttle back and the train jerked forward. I grabbed hold of the railing on the side to keep from falling backward out of the cab.

"I said *easy*," Bitter Creek repeated.

"That was easy," the engineer said. "This ain't no horse and buggy, you know. Old 457 is the biggest engine the Santa Fe has got—the biggest engine any railroad has got, period. It takes a man to control this sonuvabitch, let me tell you. If it wasn't for those guns, you reprobates would never be standing with me in this cab."

"What's his name?" I asked the fireman.

"Oscar Anderson," he said. His voice sort of squeaked. "Why?"

"I always like to know the names of the people I shoot," I explained. "It helps me keep them straight in my mind. And I've had about all the chin music I care to hear from Engineer Oscar Anderson—he's about one sentence away from getting ventilated like a sieve."

The engineer took us out to the whistle-stop with no more speeches. He brought the locomotive to a stop just short of the bridge.

"Do you have a sledgehammer up here?" I asked the fireman.

"Yes."

"Then grab it and come with us," I said.

Bitter Creek motioned with the barrel of his gun for the engineer to follow as well.

Tulsa Jack, Dynamite, and my brother Bill were walking up and down the length of the train, warning the passengers to keep their heads in. Every once in a while they would shoot over the roofs of the cars to make their point.

Doolin was waiting at the door of the Wells, Fargo car.

"The goddamned messenger won't open up," he said.

"That would be E. C. Whittlesey," the fireman said. "He's from Kansas City. He's a straight arrow, and almost as much of a pain in the butt as Anderson is."

"Whittlesey!" Doolin shouted. "Open up, son! There's no use dying for the express company! This is your last chance or we're coming in shooting!"

There was no reply from inside the car.

"Okay, boys," Doolin said. "He's been warned. Break in the door, and lay down some lead to keep our messenger's head down."

The fireman nodded, hefted the sledge, and struck the door a heavy blow. At the same time we opened up on the car, some of us with Winchesters and others with revolvers, and there was so much

noise and smoke it sounded like a war, and above all
the racket was the whine of ricochets and the tinkle
of glass breaking inside the car. Dynamite's bullets,
which were tipped with explosive, blew holes in the
sides of the express car that were the size of a man's
fist.

I used my Colt, sending slow, deliberate shots
into the car just below the roofline.

The fireman was a little skittish because of all
the lead flying around him, but kept working at the
door. While I was reloading for the third time he
broke through, and he jumped clear of the door as
if expecting Whittlesey to come out shooting.
Whittlesey, however, wasn't about to do any fighting—he was crumpled on the floor in a lake of
blood. One of the rounds had struck him in the left
hip and came out close to his backbone, just at the
belt line. He was alive, but bleeding something awful.

"Why didn't you open up?" Doolin asked,
kneeling over him. "You nearly got yourself killed."

"It's my job," he said weakly, and smiled.

Whittlesey was about twenty years old, and he
had a shock of blond hair and a pair of round wire-
framed glasses. He looked more like a schoolboy instead of a Wells, Fargo messenger.

The inside of the express car was a disaster.
There must have been a couple of hundred holes in
the walls, and splintered wood and broken glass
were everywhere. Bitter Creek found a kerosene
lamp that had survived the fusillade and lit it with a
match.

"Your job shouldn't include getting yourself
killed," Doolin told Whittlesey. "It's guys like you
that make it tough on all the rest of us. You make us
look bad. Do you think the president of the express
company would die protecting his own money?

Hell, no—this is just pocket change to him—and if he wouldn't do it, neither should you."

"I wasn't the one doing all the shooting," Whittlesey pointed out. Then he began coughing.

"No, pardner, you weren't. I told my boys to aim high, but a stray round must've gotten to you. Damn, what I don't hate strays. Can you waggle your toes?"

Doolin slipped off Whittlesey's shoes and stockings. He wiggled both of his big toes at us.

"Good," Doolin said. "You in much pain?"

"No, I just feel sort of numb."

"You will be," Doolin said. "They'll patch you up good when they get you back to town. It won't be long now. Time?"

"It's one twenty-eight," I said. "Eight minutes."

There was a cot in the back of what was left of the Wells, Fargo car, and Bitter Creek and I picked the messenger up and carried him to it. After we laid him down, Doolin demanded the key to the way safe.

"Around my neck," Whittlesey said, and lifted his head from the cot while Doolin retrieved the cord and the key that hung from it. He passed the key to Bitter Creek, who opened the safe behind us.

"Now we'll have the combination to the Wells, Fargo safe," Doolin said.

"I don't have it," Whittlesey said. "Look at it. It's one of the new burglarproof safes. All Wells, Fargo cars are being equipped with them. The combination is purposefully kept secret from the messengers. You can kill me if you want, but I don't have the combination to that safe."

Doolin walked over and stood in front of the safe. It was enormous and black as a stove, with a little round door in the center of it with a red knob for the combination. It was bolted to the floor of the express car and must have weighed more than a thousand pounds.

Doolin grasped the handle and tried to turn it, which was good thinking because the messenger could have been lying about it being locked. Unfortunately, the big ugly door wouldn't budge.

"Whittlesey," Doolin said, "are you sure about not having the combination to this safe?"

"Yes, sir," the messenger said. "Quite sure."

"We'd split it with you," Doolin said. "Nobody would ever know. You'd be a rich man, kid, and you'd never have to work another day in your life."

"No, sir, I couldn't do that, even if I knew the combination."

Doolin shook his head.

"What a waste," Doolin said. Then, to me: "Kill him."

I hesitated.

"But, boss—"

"Get rid of him," Doolin said sternly. "He's useless without the combination, and he's caused us enough trouble already. Shoot the bastard."

"Okay," I said.

I drew my revolver, knelt beside the cot, and pressed the cold barrel against Whittlesey's ear. Then I thumbed back the hammer, slow and careful, as the messenger closed his eyes and gritted his teeth. When the hammer locked into place with that last, terrifying *shnick,* a puddle of urine began forming on the floor beneath the cot.

"He really doesn't know the combination," I said, pointing the revolver up and lowering the hammer. "Sorry to make you go through that, but we had to be sure."

"Damn-it-all-to-hell," Doolin spat. "Whittlesey, you're too honest to be in this line of work. You need to find yourself another job. Have you considered applying for saint? Bitter Creek, what've you got from the way safe?"

"About a thousand dollars in silver."

"That's all?" Doolin asked.

"Yes," Whittlesey said. "That's all—a package consigned to the First National Bank of Trinidad, Colorado. There's nothing more."

"Look around," Doolin said. "There has to be something else worth taking in here."

We rummaged through the mess and looked in the stove, but there was so much paper and so many boxes scattered about that it would have taken hours to thoroughly search the car.

"Get Dynamite up here," Doolin said.

In a moment Dynamite Dick Clifton swung up into the express car with his bag of explosives.

"Can you blow that?" Doolin asked.

"I don't know," Dynamite said. "I've never seen one like it. I can give it a try." He began taking sticks of dynamite out of the sack and wedging them beneath the hinges on the door of the safe.

"Everybody out," Doolin ordered.

Bitter Creek and I picked up Whittlesey's cot and took him outside and carried him a few car lengths away. There was more shooting going on outside now as the passengers got braver and more curious about what was going on. Doolin hunkered down beside us to wait.

"It's one thirty-seven," I said. "Time to go."

"I know," Doolin said disgustedly.

Dynamite shot out of the door of the express car. He scrambled back to where we were waiting and tucked his head under his arms. The dynamite went off with a flash of orange from the open door, and the express car rocked on its springs. When the smoke inside the car had cleared, we could see that the safe was intact.

"Sorry," Dynamite said. "That's the best I can do. If there's a way to open that safe, I don't know it."

Doolin nodded and gave the order to pull out.

Bitter Creek told the engineer to wait for our signal before pulling out. They began loading Whittlesey back onboard while we mounted up and my brother Bill cut the barbed-wire fence on the south side of the railroad track. We rode off about ten rods, and Bitter Creek pulled his revolver, pointed it in the air, and fired.

The Southern California and New Mexico Express started backing away, slowly at first and then gaining speed. Its lights receded in the darkness, and its whistle began to scream a shrill warning as it neared the depot.

It was 1:45 A.M.

Two miles southeast of town we divided the loot.

Still in the saddle, Bitter Creek quickly scooped the silver coins out of the grain sack and counted out a hundred and sixty-six dollars for each of us. I was the last in line. Bitter Creek dropped a couple of dollars in the road as he handed me my share.

"Leave it," I said. "There's no time."

As agreed, Tulsa Jack and Dynamite struck out on their own. The rest of us would ride together. I dug my heels into Cimarron's flanks and led the way toward the Territory.

"Sorry, boys," Doolin shouted as we rode. "We didn't even make enough for a good drunk tonight."

We learned from the newspapers later that there had been ten thousand dollars in cash money in the way safe when the shooting started, and that Whittlesey managed to hide all but a thousand of it behind some boxes before he was plugged. The papers also said there had been a fifty-thousand-dollar payroll in the Wells, Fargo safe.

Fifteen

We crossed the Cimarron River at Deep Hole, south of Ashland, Kansas, as dawn was threatening to break on the eastern horizon. The area around Deep Hole was a weird landscape of gypsum hills and stagnant pools of water, giving way to rolling country dotted with sagebrush, soapweed, and deeply cut gullies. We reined in to almost a walk as we approached the crossing, because it was a bad place for even the surest-footed of horses; if the natural terrain weren't bad enough, hidden in the grass were the sharp ruts of three or four old cattle trails.

Instead of offering comfort, the weak half-light of the coming dawn made the shadows seem deeper and the landscape even more hellish. None of us talked as we entered the shallow water of the river, which reflected the pinks and blues of the false dawn. A pair of teal swung down over us, so low that we could hear that peculiar sound that air makes thrumming through their wings. We stopped in the middle of the river and let the horses drink. There's an old saying that you can't step in the same river twice, and I never really knew what it meant until that moment crossing the Cimarron; suddenly it became clear to me, not in words but in feelings, and I twisted in the saddle to look at my brother Bill.

If there was going to be shooting, it would start now.

There hadn't been a sign of a posse following us from Gray County, but few posses could keep up with our mounts; it was a sure bet, however, that the Gray County sheriff had telegraphed the U.S. Marshal's Office at the territorial capital of Guthrie. One of Marshal Nix's deputies—Chris Madsen, or Heck Thomas, or Bill Tilghman—had most likely put together a posse of their own, and would try to guess where we would come back into the Territory. Somebody guessed right.

As we reached the south bank of the river, a shot rang out from the west, slapping the water behind us. We pulled our Winchesters and let go with a dozen rounds or so, but it was still too dark to see anything, and the fusillade did nothing but scare the ducks from the river.

A volley answered from the dark horizon, and this time we could see their muzzle flashes. We spurred our horses on up the bank and rode south, returning fire on the fly. The worst part was not knowing how many of them there were, or who they were, or whether they were likely to give up anytime soon. Whoever they were, they either didn't have good horses or they didn't want to get too close to us, because we had put some ground between us in short order.

Then it happened. At full gallop, Cimarron's front leg caught in a prairie-dog hole and there was a terrible *crack!* as I found myself tumbling over his neck toward the ground. I instinctively put my left

arm over my head—because I knew I was going to
hit hard—and I landed squarely on a rock the size of
an eight-pound cannonball that broke both of the
bones in my forearm.

For a moment I was stunned, unable to move.
Then I rolled over onto my back and looked at the
faint stars that were disappearing from the sky.

Doolin reined Possum around.

"Bitter Creek," he shouted. "You and Bill keep
a sharp lookout for that posse while I see about the
Kid."

Doolin threw his leg over and slid down from
the saddle, his Winchester at the ready. Cimarron
was crying in pain, and Doolin checked on the horse
before he came to me.

"Cimarron?" I asked.

"Busted front leg," Doolin said. He gently
picked up my left arm. The hand was cocked at an
unnatural angle. "You, too," he said. "Can you
move your fingers?"

I could, but it hurt like hell.

"You got a pretty good knot on your punkin,
too," Doolin said. He wiped the blood from my face
with his sleeve. "You'll live, but it's going to be a
spell before we can get you patched up. Best I can
do now is make a sling for that arm."

"Okay," I said.

Doolin took my kerchief and tied it together
with his, and fitted it around my neck.

"We're going to have to move now, pardner,"
he said. "That posse is likely breathing down our
necks. Do you want to set things right, or should I?"

Tears began forming in my eyes. I couldn't help
myself.

"I'll do it," I said, but I damn near choked on
the words.

I picked up my revolver from where it had

spilled from its holster and got unsteadily to my feet. I walked over to Cimarron and knelt down beside him. The white bone of his foreleg glistened white in the darkness.

Still holding the revolver, I touched the back of my hand against his head, and despite his pain, he nuzzled back in recognition.

Then I pressed the barrel of the gun between his eyes, where the skull is thin, and pulled the trigger. I did it twice more, to be sure.

"They're coming," Bitter Creek said. "Half a mile, maybe. Soldiers and Indian scouts."

I picked up my Winchester, retrieved my loot from the saddlebag, and let my brother Bill pull me up in the saddle behind him. My arm was on fire and tears rolled down my cheeks, but not from the pain.

"You did the right thing," Bill said. "Bob would have said as much."

Then we were off again.

We headed southwest, toward the Cheyenne and Arapahoe Reserve, because Doolin reckoned the route back to Ingalls was probably filthy with marshals. We rode just hard enough to keep out of range of the posse's rifles; the Indian trackers had muzzle loaders and what the soldiers had wasn't much better. Whenever they got close enough to try their luck, we drove them back with our Winchesters.

So it went for the rest of the day, with me riding double with my brother, and Doolin and Bitter Creek keeping the posse at a comfortable distance.

Then, just above Fort Supply, we made a mistake and let the posse get ahead of us. We almost rode right into the middle of an ambush, but one of the soldiers behind a low ridge opened up too soon and gave away their position.

We exchanged a few shots with the posse, then rode to the east for the safety of a willow thicket. We were almost in the thicket—two or three hundred yards away from the posse on the ridge—when we slowed to a walk, and Doolin turned in the saddle to look behind him.

Doolin's right foot exploded in a bloody froth.

Then came the sound of the shot, rolling across the prairie behind the bullet.

Later we found out that U.S. Deputy Marshal Chris Madsen had fired the lucky shot, using his new .30-30 Winchester that fired steel-jacketed bullets.

Once in the thicket, we cut away what was left of Doolin's right boot and studied the damage. The bullet had struck him in the heel and followed the arch to the ball of the foot, where it had busted things up good. A couple of his toes were hanging by strips of skin.

"Damn," Doolin said. "Shot right where my mother held on to me when she dipped me in Big Piney back home in Arkansas."

Sixteen

We were in something of a fix. Doolin's foot was busted up so from Chris Madsen's lucky shot that he couldn't walk and could just barely ride. My broken arm wasn't so bad, except I wouldn't be a whole lot of good in a fight, once I had thumbed and fired all six rounds in my pistol—it would take a long time to reload because, with the use of only one hand, I would have to break the gun open and lay it on the ground to shove the shells into it. And somewhere behind us was Madsen and his posse of soldiers and scouts, just spoiling to get us at a disadvantage.

"Let's stand and fight," my brother Bill said.

"No," Doolin said. "We'll split up."

"Good," I said. "It's nearly dark, and that will help."

"Bitter Creek," Doolin said. "You take off and we'll hook up in a few days at Ingalls. Bill, you'd best make a beeline for your ma's house near Kingfisher, and keep your head down once you're there. Since we're the cripples, the Kid and I will stick together and do the best we can."

133

"We can't leave you," Bitter Creek said.

"You had better," Doolin said, "because I'd just slow you down and make it so we all get caught."

"Well, that's not fair to the Kid," Bill said.

"The hell it ain't," I said. "We've only got three horses. What Doolin says makes sense. And we don't have a lot of time, so I suggest you two get moving."

I grabbed the back of Doolin's belt with my good hand and pulled myself up into the saddle behind him.

Bill touched a forefinger to the brim of his hat and rode out.

"See you in Ingalls," Bitter Creek said, and did the same.

Doolin dug his heels into Possum's flanks and steered us rangeward. He knew that the posse would end up following the deep blood-flecked tracks—ours, that is—just as you would follow the tracks of a deer that you whanged but did not kill. Darkness gave us some advantage, but it did not make up for two wounded men on a single horse.

We headed southwest, and we crossed the North Canadian three or four miles ahead of the soldiers and Indian scouts. Behind us on the rolling plain we got occasional glimpses of the posse, as the scouts used lanterns to stop and read the sign. Through the night those lights kept moving closer and closer. Doolin was in a considerable amount of pain, and about midnight he told me that he was finished unless we could find someplace to hide. He was slipping in and out, and his eyes were open only part of the time.

I was searching for a high piece of ground upon which to make a stand when I spied the glow of a light inside a tent below us on the Ivanhoe, where it empties into Wolf Creek, a quarter of a mile away.

"Come on," I told Doolin. "Let's investigate."

"Could be lawmen," Doolin said heavily.

"Then we'll have the advantage of surprise," I said.

As we drew closer we could see that there was not one tent, but three, although only the lighted one seemed to be occupied at the moment. They were the peculiar conical tents used by the military and sometimes by cowboys. From the gear that was laying around, the branding irons and saddles, and the horses nearby, it was clear that this was a cow camp.

"What now?" Doolin asked.

"We're going to borrow one of these unoccupied tents for a spell," I said, slipping down off the horse. Then I helped Doolin down, and although his right foot never touched the ground, I could hear him grind his teeth against the pain.

"What about Possum?" I asked.

"Don't worry about him," Doolin said. "He'll blend in with their remuda and stay close until I need him."

"Your horse sounds smarter than most people I know," I said.

"No," Doolin said, "but he's a damn sight more honest."

With Doolin leaning on my good arm, we limped around the nearest tent to the opening. Then I drew my revolver and moved the flap aside with the barrel, ready for a fight at any moment. The tent, however, was as deserted as it appeared.

"Roy?" a voice called from the lighted tent.

Doolin and I sort of fell in through the opening and lay on the floor of the tent, trying not to move a muscle.

We could hear the sound of a man leaving the other tent and walking about outside. Footsteps approached the front of our tent.

"You come back early, Roy?" the voice asked.

Then, after what seemed like an eternity:

"Damn, I guess I'm hearing things."

The man went back to his own tent.

Doolin and I started breathing again. We untangled ourselves and moved to either side of the tent, which was just as small as it had looked. The good thing is that it had plenty of blankets inside, and we burrowed beneath them, partly to hide, and partly for warmth. Even though it was June, both of us were freezing.

"What happens when they find us?" Doolin asked.

I didn't have an answer.

Soon we were asleep, pistols in our hands.

I opened my eyes and it took me a few minutes to figure out that I was looking up into tent canvas, with daylight shining through the weave. My whole body was stiff and my left arm throbbed with pain, keeping time with the bass drum in my temples.

"Howdy."

I tried to lift my head up from the floor, but my neck was so stiff I couldn't immediately manage it. I noted that my Colt had been removed from my right hand.

"To hell with it," I said. "Shoot me and get it over with. Right here, where the skull is the thinnest. Then do it twice more to make sure."

"I ain't going to shoot you," the man said.

I rolled over on my side so I could get a look at him.

The cowboy was kneeling, but I could tell from the way his head brushed the roof of the tent that he was tall. He had dark brown eyes and a dark, flowing mustache, and even though he was young—he didn't look twenty-five yet—he was going bald on top. A cigarette hung from the corner of his mouth. He was working on Doolin's foot in his lap. There was a washbasin, a bottle of whiskey, and a pile of bloody rags on the floor. Doolin's head was thrown back and he looked dead to the world.

"Who are you?" I asked.

"Roy Daugherty."

"Where are we?"

"This is the Box T range of the Dominion Cattle Company. I'm not with the outfit. I'm just camped here rounding up some lost steers from a stampede we had the other night during a thunderstorm. Do you want a smoke?"

I nodded.

Daugherty stopped doctoring Doolin's foot for a moment and pulled his bag of makings out. In a moment he had rolled a quirly, lit it, and handed it to me.

"Well, I'll bet you're wondering who the hell we are," I said after I took a long drag, and started in with an unlikely story about some honest drovers who got caught in a stampede.

"Don't lie," the cowboy said. "Mr. Doolin here spilled most of it while he was out of his head last night. The rest I can fill in. You're the Choctaw Kid, and along with some other friends you hit the Santa Fe at Cimarron. It's been in all the papers. 'Gentlemanly Bandits,' that's what they call you."

"Is that bottle strictly for medicinal purposes?"

Daugherty found a tin cup and poured it full of whiskey.

"At least I won't die from snakebite," I said after taking a drink. "Whittlesey. The messenger—did he live?"

"Yes," he said. "Seems to me that the *New West* said he was going back to Kansas City to recuperate, and it's believed he'll be back on the job in four weeks."

I nodded. "What about the posse?" I asked.

"There were some marshals through here early this morning," the cowboy said. "But I told them I hadn't seen anybody. Seeing as how Mr. Doolin and myself both come from Arkansas, it just seemed the neighborly thing to do. What're you going to do now?"

"Try to get back to Ingalls, where Doolin can get some help."

"There are doctors closer than that," he said.

"None that Doolin trusts," I said. "He has a powerful fear of a doctor killing him on the operating table for the reward money. He carries five thousand dollars on his head, you know."

"Well, now," Daugherty said. "I am somewhat tired of the cowboy life. I was enamored of it when I was a kid, having been sheltered and coming from a family of preachers and all. My ma died when I was young, and my stepmother was a holy terror with a hickory switch, so I lit out when I was fourteen."

"Thirteen or fourteen does seem the age for it," I said.

"I went to Texas and became a right good cowboy," said Daugherty. "But after ten years of the life, it does not seem so glamorous. There's no pay to speak of, and what you do get you end up putting into your rig or blowing it all at the end of the trail. Besides, it's harder to find work now than ever, and in September, all of this—the whole Cherokee Strip—will be gone, cut up, fenced off, plowed up, and closed down. No, sir, I've had enough of being a cowboy."

"What do you want to be now?"

"An outlaw," he said, and the corners of his mustache rose with his grin.

"I think that can be arranged," I said, "although I can't truly recommend the work. But I'm sure Doolin will be appreciative of your efforts on his behalf. Do you think you can help me get him back to Ingalls?"

Daugherty nodded.

"We'll need some horses," he said. "I can steal some good mounts from the remuda here. Sort of look at it as back pay, if you know what I mean."

"No, don't steal anything here," I said. "If you've got your own horse, all we need is one more. Do you think your trail boss will sell one?"

"It's possible," he said.

"Well, I've got a hundred and sixty-four dollars. It will have to do."

"What do you want?"

"The best and fastest I can get for the money," I said. "But anything right now is better than walking. And you'd better do it before you quit, or he's likely to be a little frothy. You savvy?"

Daugherty nodded.

"What do you want me to call you?" I asked.

"What do you mean?"

"I'm sure you don't want to use your real name, out of consideration for that family of preachers back home, if nothing else," I said, and finished off the cup of whiskey. "What do you want to be your alias? All the best outlaws have one."

Daugherty thought on it for a minute.

"Well, I was born in Arkansas, and I became a

cowboy in Tom Green County, Texas. So why don't you call me Arkansas Tom Green?"

"Yeah," I said. "That fits. But you seem to be kind of a rake, so let's add some dash to it. Let's make it Arkansas Tom Jones."

Seventeen

The best and fastest horse Arkansas Tom could get from the trail boss was a swaybacked wreck named Rumbleguts that looked like it had seen its prime at some point during the War Between the States. It was a mean-spirited beast that tried to bite me every chance it got. Still, it was good enough to get back on the trail with. Doolin's foot was festering something awful and we had to get him to Ingalls, where it could be doctored.

On a good day it would have taken a day or two to make it back. But thanks to Doolin's bad foot, and my bum arm, it took us a week, even with Arkansas Tom's help. The Territory seemed to be crawling with lawmen, all waiting to get a shot at Bill Doolin and his Wild Bunch.

We rode mostly at night, slept on the ground, and when we had food we ate it cold. During the day we would lay low, in some brush or alongside a creek, and talk or play cards. We were two days out from Ingalls, I remember, hiding out in an old barn when Doolin told me that for the first time in his life, he was scared.

"What d'you mean, Bill?" I asked.

"Kid, I could take this life when it was just me," he said. "But now I have a wife waiting for me back home. Hell, I feel like I've hardly been able to see her since we got married. I'm not scared for myself, I'm scared for her. It ain't no life for a lady. And what happens if we have a kid? How long do you think I've got?"

"I don't know," I said. "You could go quite awhile yet."

"Well, I grew up not knowing my own father," Doolin said. "He was a sharecropper who worked himself to death by the time I was seven, but he bought us our own farm before he died, and it was a good one. I don't think I should ever have left there. I think of how nice things would have worked out if only I could take Edith there, and I could live out the rest of my years in peace. But it ain't going to happen."

"Bill?" I asked.

"What?"

"I don't mean you to take this wrong, but how many people have you killed?"

Doolin laughed.

"I ain't killed nobody, least not that I know about," he said. "I've winged some folks, that's for sure. But I've seen people shot, seen people I trusted up and kill innocent folks for the hell of it. And I've seen folks kilt for no good reason at all, from stray bullets and such. That's what I worry about. Them strays. What if I've killed somebody without knowing it, somebody that meant me absolutely no harm? That's really worse than killing on purpose somebody who's laying for you. . . . Kid, do you believe in God?"

"That's a complicated question, Bill."

"Either you do or you don't. What in hell is so complicated?"

"Well," I said, "I cannot believe that Jesus Christ was the Son of God, but I reckon that His teachings are about the best we've had. We sure seem to pile up misery for ourselves when we go against them. But I can't tolerate religious people, because they're forcing their opinions on you from the cradle to the grave. I don't like to force my opinions on anybody. And their view of God—a vengeful, all-powerful father—sticks in my craw. Why can't God be . . . well, nice? So to answer your question, I would like to believe in God, but a God who is sort of a good father instead of an asshole."

"That's the damnedest way of saying so I ever heard. Point is, what do you reckon God is going to say to me when He gets me up there at those pearly gates? Is He going to say, 'Bill Doolin, you can rot in hell for what you done'?"

"I don't know," I said. "I'm not God. But I tell you one thing—my God would give you a good listen and a fair shake, that's for sure."

"I hope you're right," Doolin said. "I ain't really scared of dying, and I'm not really ashamed of much I've done. There's just one thing that boogers me bad."

"What's that?"

"I don't want to be buried in no potter's grave," Doolin said, fingering the checkering on the forestock of his Winchester. "I don't want to lie with Judas for eternity. I have night sweats about my grave being forgot and trampled by animals."

Doolin sighed.

"Nothing I can do about any of it, I reckon."

• • •

By the time we got back to Ingalls I was twenty
pounds lighter and my clothes hung off me like I
was some kind of scarecrow. We came dragging
down Second Street about midnight, and all the
lights were out in the shops and houses along the
way.

Lucinda met me in the middle of the street.

"I knew you were back," she said. "I could feel
you."

I slid down from the saddle and took her in my
arms.

"Lucky," I said, "I've missed your wicked
smile."

We hugged each other for a few more moments,
then I introduced her to Arkansas Tom, who tipped
his hat. Then I briefly described the hell we had
gone through since the Cimarron holdup, and asked
her to go wake up Doc Selph to work on Doolin's
foot.

It took quite a while for Doc to pick out all the
little chips of bone and other trash that was inside
the infected foot, then he cleaned it out with car-
bolic acid and said Doolin should be able to walk
again in a week or two, if he stayed off it for now.

Then it was my turn.

My left arm wasn't healing right—it was more
than a little crooked and hurt like hell when anybody touched it—and Selph had to break it again so
he could reset it straight. I drank half a bottle of
whiskey beforehand, but it still felt like he was tearing my arm off when he did it. He put my arm in a
sling and told me to keep it still until he told me not
to.

Then I went over to the O.K. Hotel and slept.
Lucinda sat on a chair next to the bed, and watched
from the window to make sure that no lawmen rode
into town.

• • •

I slept the whole day through and woke the next morning feeling starved. But I was broke—at least until I went out to my backwoods bank and withdrew a little of the money that was stashed there—so Lucinda had to loan me enough money to pay for breakfast at the Nix Restaurant, where I ate a heap of ham and eggs and drank about a gallon of coffee.

Then I went over to the livery and collected Rumbleguts for the ride out to the woods. The boy, Del Simmons, asked me what had happened to Cimarron.

"Dead," I said. "Broke his leg, and I had to kill him."

The boy nodded sadly.

"Why does it always happen to the good ones?" he asked.

I didn't know.

Lucinda accompanied me, on a little dun-colored mare rented from the livery. The boy had asked her if she wanted a sidesaddle, and she laughed.

It was a good day to ride. It was late June, the sky was clear, and the weather was not yet too hot. Rumbleguts only nipped at me once. We took our time getting to the place where I had hidden the money among the stones. When I dug it up I took the whole poke, which amounted to a few hundred dollars.

"Let's spread your bedroll out," Lucinda said.

"Why?" I asked.

She gave me a look that said I can be pretty thick at times.

I took the tarp and spread it out where the ground looked the most even. Lucinda began pulling off her clothes, and when she was completely shucked she crawled over to me and kissed me softly on the mouth. "We have to be careful of your arm," she said. We were beneath a canopy of trees, and I remembered looking up into their branches and feeling the warm earth beneath my shoulders as we made love.

We stopped on the way back through town at Dr. Call's Pharmacy, on Second Street across from the O.K. Hotel, so Lucinda could buy a couple of bottles of laudanum. While she was doing that I poked through the trash they had on the shelves out front and came up with a box of candy, which I paid for and tucked beneath my good arm.

"What've you got?" Lucinda asked as we stepped outside onto the plank sidewalk.

I didn't get a chance to answer.

Something jumped out from between the buildings just in front of us, a hulking something with a face that looked as if it had been run through a buzz saw and stitched back together, and I saw the gaping twin barrels of an eight-gauge shotgun being brought to bear upon us. The hammers on both barrels were cocked, and at this range, it was sure to kill us both—and probably anybody who might be standing within ten feet on either side.

For a moment I felt frozen, rooted to the spot. My fanning hand was done up in a sling and my good trigger hand was clutching a box of candy beneath my arm. I shouldered Lucinda hard, knocking her off the sidewalk and into the street.

Then I did the only thing that seemed natural.

I slung the box of candy at the assassin.

The box was aimed at his face, and as he flinched he brought the shotgun up, jerking both triggers. The hammers fell and the eight-gauge sounded like a cannon as a double load of buckshot burst open the box of candy and chewed up the wood above my head on the underside of the covered porch. Bits of candy wrapped in party-colored papers fell at our feet.

My Colt was coming out of its holster now, a mite slower than usual because I didn't have the use of my left hand and arm, which helps the rhythm, but it was fast enough because he was standing there with an empty shotgun. His mouth dropped open as I thumbed back the hammer and blew his brains out the back of his head. The force of the bullet nearly lifted him out of his boots and laid him out backward onto the board sidewalk.

I whirled, expecting a friend or some kin of his to come at me from behind, but the sidewalk was clear. He had apparently been alone.

Some folks were craning their heads out of the doorways of the shops along Second Street to see what the shooting was about. Lucinda was sitting on her rump in the street.

I broke open the loading gate of the Colt and ejected the spent shell, plucked a fresh one from my belt, and shoved it home. Then I holstered my gun and went over to inspect the man I had killed.

It was Darlington.

I should have made sure he was dead when they carried him away in the wagon after the fight in the saloon. His face had healed badly, and looked as if it had been treated by some backwoods power doctor who just made the scarring worse. He was so ugly that I'm sure children ran when they saw him. I know I wanted to.

It had been stupid of me to cut his face after I had won the fight in Vaughn's saloon, and that act of stupidity had come back and nearly cost me and Lucinda our lives. Not that I felt bad about killing

him now—no, he deserved it, after all he had done
to Lucinda. But meanness has a way of coming back
to haunt you, and in my guts I knew the killing
wasn't done yet.

I scooped up some of the candy, walked over to
Lucinda, and helped her up. She brushed the red
dust from her dress and remarked that the road was
harder than it looked.

"Is he dead?" she asked. "I mean, you're sure
this time."

I described for her the condition of his head.

She nodded grimly.

"Piece of candy?" I asked.

When we returned to the livery, Del told me that
there had been a man there asking questions about
horseshoes.

"Yeah," I said. "Big guy with his face all
chopped up."

"No," the boy said. "This fellow was medium
height, and rather handsome. He seemed like a marshal to me."

"Oh?"

"Yes. He was asking about this horseshoe he
carried with him in his pocket, about where it had
been made and so on. It was one of Mr. Light's
shoes, Choctaw. He's an artist of a blacksmith and
his shoes are very distinctive. . . . I think the shoe
was taken from Cimarron."

"What did you tell him?" I asked.

"Well, he showed me the shoe first, you know,
just real friendly. Talked about how it was stock Di-
amond shoe with Cape Well nails, but that it had
been worked special by somebody who knew what
they were doing. I told him it was indeed Mr. Light's
work. Then he started asking me questions about all

the horses that have been shod here, and their riders, and whether any of them rode a blood bay with this patch that looked like a thunderbolt on its forehead, and I realized he was talking about you, Choctaw. I shut up, then, but I'm afraid it was too late. Jesus, I'm sorry."

The boy was about to cry.

"Don't worry about it, Del," I said. "They would have tracked that shoe down sooner or later. It's not your fault. Besides, it's best to tell the truth when you can. Don't be like me. Do you understand?"

He nodded.

"Where is this could-be-a-marshal fellow now?"

"I don't know," Del said. "He came and left just after you and Miss ... Miss ... after you and Lucky rode out this morning."

"I'm going away for a spell," I told him. "Would you put Rumbleguts up for me? And try to sell him if you can. I hate that damn horse."

I gave the boy five dollars.

"Where will you go?" Lucinda asked me.

"Eureka Springs. Folks come there from all over to take the baths and a couple of new faces aren't likely to be noticed. Besides, it might help my arm to heal."

She thought for a moment.

Then she asked, "A *couple* of faces?"

Eighteen

We became different people in Eureka Springs.

Once we stepped off the train in the little mountain town in northwestern Arkansas, it felt as though some great weight had been lifted from our shoulders. Dressed as I was in my Prince Albert and derby hat, with a wad of greenbacks in my pocket and Lucinda on my arm, none of the people we met on the street could have guessed that I was a gunslinger for the Wild Bunch.

Nobody knew anything about us, except for the air of respectability that we projected, and there was comfort in that friendly anonymity that passes between strangers on holiday. I smoked big cigars and carried a cane. Folks complimented us on our obvious success in business, because we seemed so young.

We were "Mr. and Mrs. Smith, from Little Rock," and when people asked how I made my money, I said "banking." Lucinda just smiled tightly. I kept my revolver and gun belt rolled up in a suitcase at our hotel, and carried instead a small

.32-caliber pistol in a shoulder holster beneath my jacket. We ate at the best restaurants and we soaked in the steaming mineral waters at the bathhouses and generally behaved like royalty. My arm began to knit, and although the bones still pained me some, I discarded the sling entirely.

Our second morning in Eureka Springs, we walked downtown for breakfast and chanced to pass the storefront of R. Flagg, Dentist. The storefront was plastered with testimonials to his skill at "painless dentistry" and his expertise at fitting appliances to fill gaps in teeth.

Lucinda looked at me.

"Let's go in and see what he has to say," I said.

R. Flagg was a thin man with bad skin and splayed hands that looked like a raccoon's. He was sitting in his dental chair, reading the *Police Gazette*, and he jumped up with such vitality that we paused on the threshold, unsure if it was safe to venture farther.

"Come in, come in," he urged with a wave of his paw. "What can I do for such a distinguished-looking pair today?" When he saw Lucinda's smile he uttered a little "Oh" and all but carried her to the chair.

"Open up, dear," he said pleasantly.

Lucinda did, and he promptly stuck into her mouth something that looked like a walnut pick and another something that seemed like a tiny vanity mirror.

"Ah," Flagg said. "How did you lose this tooth, dear?"

Lucinda tried to explain, but his hardware was still in her mouth. Her eyes were wide, but not as wide as Flagg had her mouth stretched.

"These others are in dreadful shape as well. Were you often given calomel as a child for, say, the treatment of typhoid, yellow fever, or dysentery?"

Lucinda gave a little nod.

"Yes, I thought so," he said. "The mercury in that agent destroys the bones of the jaw, resulting in loss of teeth. It can cause a person quite a bit of pain. From the shape of these teeth, I can see you've been suffering for some time. Many people are forced to rely on laudanum or some other patent medicine whose active ingredient is an opiate."

He withdrew the tools from her mouth.

"Can you do anything to fix her up?" I asked.

"Well, it's not that simple," Flagg said. "You see, the jaw has been destroyed where the tooth came out. It is not a simple matter of filling a hole, but of building a bridge between her good teeth on either side. That will require some grinding and shaping with the chisels and the hand drill."

"It sounds painful," I said.

"Frankly, it *is* uncomfortable," Flagg admitted. "But we can administer Acestoria, a local anesthetic composed of various oils and one-percent cocaine."

"What do you think?" Lucinda asked.

"It's your mouth," I said.

"Doc, how much will all this fancy masonry cost?" she asked.

He coughed into his sleeve and thought a moment before answering. "Approximately one hundred dollars," he said carefully. "The process will take at least three separate visits, over the course of a week or two."

"What do you think, Sam?" she asked. "It's so much money."

"Why not?" I said. "You're worth it."

Flagg said he studied—at considerable personal expense—with an established dentist in Fort Smith the year before to learn his trade, and that he was sure he could handle this routine job. So I handed him half of the money and he scheduled an appointment for the next day to begin work.

Lucinda went back for three more times, and each time she came back to the hotel she looked worse, as if somebody had worked her face over with a hammer. She was bruised from the tops of her cheekbones to the tip of her chin. Finally, when it was all over, she had the gap in her smile filled, despite looking like she had gone a few rounds with Mike Fink. If you ignored the bruises you could hardly tell there was anything wrong with Lucinda's smile, if you didn't know which part of it was porcelain.

She kept the new tooth in her mouth all the time for a spell, even to bed, and I was afraid she would choke on the damn thing during the middle of the night. Then she started leaving it out once in a while, to give her mouth a rest, she said, and pretty soon she was leaving it out most of the time because she complained it hurt too much when it was in. Eventually it just stayed on the night table by the bed.

One morning in our hotel room, while I was sitting on the balcony overlooking Basin Street, reading the newspaper and drinking coffee, Lucinda came and sat beside me. We had been in Eureka Springs for nearly a month. She put her hand on my arm, as if she wanted to tell me something of great importance.

"Sam," she said. "I've never been this happy."

The truth was, neither had I.

Lucinda started to cry, and she leaned her head against my shoulder as the tears rolled down her cheeks. She sniffled a bit, but she didn't sob.

"You know," she said, "I grew up in an orphanage on the southeast corner of Seventeenth and Grandview in Kansas City. My mother was a whore who gave me up for adoption when I was three months old."

"Is Lucinda your real name?"

"No," she said.

"Then what is?"

"I won't tell you. That is behind me now and I don't want to be reminded of it. I hated the orphanage. There was no warmth there—it was like a prison, only the inmates were children, not criminals. The building itself froze in the winter, the girls were mean, and we never had enough to eat.

"The children were treated like animals, and as soon as we were old enough to carry a broom or a mop, we were put to work. The people who ran the place cared only about money. That's why I married to get out of there, just as soon as I could. Of course, my husband beat me, and I was in no better shape than in the orphanage, so I ran away from him. Eventually I wound up with Darlington, and you know what happened from there.

"You know what I liked to do at the orphanage? Well, as long as the weather would allow, I would sit outside, next to the big iron fence that surrounded the place, and watch all the people as they passed by with business downtown, people who look like we do now.

"They looked so happy, and I invented stories in my head about who they were and where they were going. Such as, well, 'There goes old Mrs. Shortridge, and she's off to pick up her son Ludwig at the music conservatory, where he is studying piano.' Or, 'There is dear Mr. Crispin, he's the best attorney in town, and he is on his way to file some legal papers that will shut this place down.' Silly trash, really, but it was a way to keep myself from going crazy."

I nodded.

"There was a nun who used to come visit us at the orphanage from time to time, and I used to count the days until her next visit, because she was so kind to me and acted so much like the mother I never had. Her name was Mary. Do you know what she used to tell me when I was discouraged? She'd say, 'Don't cry—things will get better.' Then she would tell me, 'Where there is life, there is hope.' And now I realize that she was right."

She kissed me on the cheek.

"Sam, I'm swearing off whoring," she said. "I know now how much I love you. This past month has been wonderful. Let's get married."

I just smiled and squeezed her hand, because I didn't have the sand to tell her that our money was about gone. We would soon have to go back to being the people we really were. They say that money can't buy happiness, but I reckon that most people just haven't found the right store.

Nineteen

The summer burned away like a slow fuse.

We shouldn't have returned to Ingalls—looking back, there probably were a hundred other places we could have gone—but at the time we thought we had no choice. No money in your pocket will do that to you, will make you think you're painted into the worst corner you've ever seen, and you'll likely do something to make that fear come true.

Still, we tried to make the best of it. Lucinda moved out of Sadie Comley's and in with Edith Doolin, who since her marriage had lived in a little white house along Second Street, near the O.K. Hotel.

Doolin was rarely around, since he believed his presence was a danger to Edith, and he slept at the Rock Fort or sometimes at the hotel. When he visited his bride it was in the dead of night, and always with his Winchester within handy reach. He never left Possum tied out front, but always put him up at the stable beforehand. It was a strange arrangement. Doolin's marriage to Edith was a secret to all but the most trusted gang members, so the couple's nocturnal activity was the subject of a lot of gossip in Ingalls that summer.

Lucinda and I planned to get hitched just as soon as I managed to save a little money and had broken Emmett out of jail. After that, I said, I could retire from the outlaw trail and we could live like normal people.

Del had no luck in selling Rumbleguts—in fact, he couldn't give the nag away. So I was stuck with a horse whose dearest wish was to bite away a pound or two of my flesh, and I couldn't even pay for the feed it used.

With things so tight, it wasn't long before Lucinda started complaining and I started drinking. How could we afford to get married, she asked, when I couldn't support us even though I was in the most famous outlaw gang in the country? I spent my time in Ransom and Murray's saloon, throwing shots of whiskey down my gut on credit and waiting for Doolin to pronounce that it was time for the Wild Bunch to pull another job.

But Doolin never did.

He kept saying it was too hot, that things had to simmer down some before we went back to work. So I drank more, fought with Lucinda, and cleaned my idle guns.

Toward the end of July, a railroad survey crew pitched its tents not far from the saloon, and it wasn't long before the surveyors were a regular fixture at Doolin's poker table. The senior man was named Red Lucas—he had flaming red hair and mustache—and the other fellow was named Roberts. They were mediocre gamblers but seemed friendly enough; they were polite and always seemed interested in chatting about what Doolin and the fellows were up to.

In the middle of August, President Cleveland announced that the Cherokee Strip, all eight million acres of it, would be up for grabs in a land run that would start at noon on September 16. There had been land runs in Oklahoma Territory before, but this one promised to be the biggest and the last. Boomers started pouring into the Territory from all directions, and Ingalls was a particular favorite destination, since northern Payne County had been declared as one of the spots where the run would start.

All this excitement about free land gave me an idea—why couldn't Lucinda and I stake a little claim? I could retire from bank and train robbery and become a farmer, like my older brothers. The problem was, I didn't have a dime to my name, and there were going to be certain expenses involved, at the land office and such. And Rumbleguts wasn't much of a horse for a land run. I needed a new horse as well.

So I had Doolin stake me ten dollars and I waited that evening in the saloon for Lucas and Roberts to make their nightly visit. I didn't tell Lucinda about my plan, because I wanted to surprise her. I waited at the bar, sipping at my beer, waiting for the surveyors. Finally they came in, joking with the boys good-naturedly, and sat down with Doolin at the poker table.

"Whose deal?" Lucas asked in his Irish brogue.

Doolin held up his hands.

"Sorry," he said. "I'm done for today. I've lost enough money."

"That's a shame," Lucas said. "We're ready to play." He turned and asked over his shoulder, "Anybody else interested in a few hands?"

Nobody in the saloon answered.

I placed my empty beer glass carefully upon the bar.

"I wouldn't mind sitting in," I said.

Lucas motioned me over. I sat down where Doolin had just been.

"It's a dollar ante," Lucas said.

I put a silver dollar on the table and Lucas began to shuffle the cards. "So," he said as he began to click out five cards to each of us, "I've noticed you around the saloon quite a bit lately. You live around here?"

"Uh-huh," I said, examining my cards. It was not a particularly good beginning. I had a pair of nines and nothing else.

"Known Doolin long?"

"Long enough," I said.

Roberts upped the ante another dollar. Lucas put in his dollar, and after a moment's hesitation, so did I. Roberts threw back one card, Lucas sent back two, and I pushed three toward the discard pile.

Lucas dealt the new cards. There was another nine in my stack.

Roberts put another dollar in. Lucas folded. After deliberating some, I placed another dollar in the pot.

"What've you got?" I asked.

He laid down a full house, jacks and queens. I threw my cards facedown and Roberts raked in the pot. We put our dollars in for the ante and it was my turn to deal.

I gathered the cards and shuffled them. It had been a spell since I had a deck of cards in my hands, and it showed. I offered the cut to Roberts, on my right.

He refused.

I dealt the cards.

"How long have you ridden with Doolin?" Lucas asked as he studied his cards. "Were you with him on the Cimarron job?"

"No. Were you?" I asked. Lucas was beginning to annoy me. I had two pair, aces and eights.

"Why, of course not," he said, smiling. "I was just trying to make conversation, friend. What do folks call you around here?"

"They call me 'Kid.' "

"Okay, Kid, that's all I wanted to know." He upped the ante by two dollars. I was in and so was Roberts. "Gimme two cards."

I did. Roberts took three and I drew one—another ace. It made a full house. I couldn't tell by their expressions what luck Lucas and Roberts had.

"What railroad are you with?" I asked.

Roberts pumped another dollar into the pot.

"The Katy," he said.

"That's funny," I said, shelling out my money. "I didn't think the Kansas, Missouri, and Texas came this far west into the Territory. I'll raise you fellows three dollars." It was the last of my money.

"Oh, it will," Lucas said. "We're scouting a new route."

"It must be a short one," I said. "You fellows never seem to get very far from Ingalls."

"I'm out," Roberts said, and threw his cards on the table.

"Well, we like to keep our camp near a town, for the convenience of the thing. What've you got, friend?"

"Full house," I said, and spread the hand on the table.

Lucas looked at the cards and whistled.

"That's a mighty fine hand, Choctaw," he said. "But it don't beat four of a kind."

He laid four kings and a deuce on the table.

"Sorry," he said, gathering in the money. "Would you like to go another round?"

I started at him. Then I pushed my chair back

away from the table, to have enough room to get my gun up and out if I needed to.

"How'd you know they call me Choctaw?" I asked.

"Huh? Oh," he said, smiling broadly beneath his red mustache. "I guess I must have heard it one night, and it didn't come to me until just now. There's no reason to become angry, partner. I won't forget your name again."

"I'll bet you never have," I said. "And what about all those questions about how long I've ridden with Doolin and such? What kind of trash was that? You sure as hell aren't surveyors, are you?"

"Of course we are," Roberts said. "You can come out to our camp and look at our equipment. I swear."

Roberts was spooked, but Lucas was still a little cocky. My hand was hanging down near the butt of my Colt, and I was watching both of them carefully for any movement that might mean they were reaching for their guns.

"Sit down, son," Lucas said. "You're making a fool of yourself. . . . You didn't lose that much money."

"It ain't the money," I said. "You are Pinkerton agents or worse. You'd best clear out of here before I fill you full of lead."

Well, it *was* the money. Losing that ten dollars made me uncontrollably angry. I wanted to shoot both of them, dead. And I knew they weren't railroad surveyors. But that isn't why I wanted to kill them. I wanted to kill them because I *lost*.

Roberts got out of his chair and backed away for the door.

Lucas was a mite cockier. He cleared his throat and carefully put his winnings in his pocket. Then he drained the last of his beer and put his glass down on the table. His coat had fallen back to reveal the butt of an ivory-handled Smith & Wesson.

"You know, if I wanted to—"

My Colt was cocked and aimed at his nose before he even knew what happened. He stood there, his eyes staring down at the barrel of my revolver.

"You'd what?" I asked.

"Nothing," he said. "Never mind."

He followed his partner to the door.

We didn't see Lucas or Roberts again after that, at least not in the saloon. Doolin later said he had been suspicious of them, but they seemed nice enough.

That night Lucinda called off the marriage.

She said I was just another drunken outlaw and that I never would manage to break my brother out of the Kansas Penitentiary at Lansing and that I would never have enough money for us to get married. She reckoned she was losing a fortune in what she was giving away to me. She said she was going back to her chosen profession, and that I could see her at her room at Sadie Comley's anytime I wanted—for two dollars.

So I marched over to the saloon and proceeded to get tight as a brick. After an hour or so I stumbled out the front door of the saloon and stumbled down Second Street, past Sadie Comley's and the O.K. Hotel, to Pickering's Grove. There were a couple hundred boomer families camped down there, with their wagons and their household goods and their squalling kids, waiting for the opening of the Cherokee Strip. The run was still a couple of weeks off, but the boomers had been slipping across the line and scouting out west, and most of them already knew the piece of land they was going to aim for.

I pulled my Colt and fired into the air to get their attention.

Everything got real quiet. Then the women and kids scattered and the men came out of their tents and wagons with old shotguns and single-shot rifles to see what the trouble was. In a flash I was surrounded by loaded guns, but I didn't give a damn.

"Go home!" I shouted.

I had been prepared to give a speech about how they were ruining everything, that Oklahoma Territory had enough civilization already, that they ought to leave it to the Indians and the outlaws. Trouble was, I couldn't seem to form any of the words to convey that message. So I stood in the middle of them, more than a little unsteady on my feet, my six-gun still in hand.

"Go home!" I shouted again.

"Hell," one of the grangers said, then spit a wad of tobacco on the ground. "Ain't nothing but another drunk cowboy. Put your gun down, son, before you hurt somebody."

The man was old, probably about forty, and his face was gaunt and spiderwebbed with worry lines. There was no fear in his eyes. He didn't know who I was, or about my reputation, and he obviously didn't care. I am ashamed to admit that for a moment I thought about killing him, even though I knew the others would cut me down.

The urge passed. I holstered my gun.

I thought I hated these men, and their wives of twenty years, and their dreams. I thought I hated them for their small lives and their pathetic plans, for never making the newspapers and never having anybody tremble in fear or anticipation at the mention of their names.

But I was wrong.

I hated myself for not being like them, for choosing a gun instead of the plow. I hated myself for becoming a drunk and for being mean-spirited enough to abuse them from the middle of their own camp. But mostly I hated myself for being relieved that Lucinda had called the wedding off, because I knew she was right—because of me, we could never have a normal life.

I passed out. Somebody was kind enough to drag me beneath one of the wagons and throw a blanket over me.

Twenty

I have never been partial to Fridays.

Maybe it has something to do with Friday being hangman's day or—if you believe in that sort of truck—the day that Our Lord was nailed to the cross. It just naturally seemed to be a day of suffering to me, and what happened on this particular Friday—the first of September, 1893—just confirmed that belief.

First of all, I had a terrific hangover.

It was cold overnight, and fog invaded the low places, and when I woke up I felt like hell warmed over and didn't know where I was because everything was wrapped in a white blanket.

So I stayed shivering beneath the wagon and waited until the sun came up and started burning away the mist before I laid the blanket aside and crawled out.

I made my way stiffly back up the hill to Second Street. After brushing myself off as best I could, I went to the O.K. Hotel and climbed the stairs to the attic, where the cowhands stayed. The attic was unfinished—there wasn't even a ceiling hiding the peaked roof—and you could see daylight between some of the boards, where the shingles had come loose. But the attic did have a few items of comfort, such as a half-dozen beds and some scattered pieces of furniture.

Mrs. Pierce had heard me come up the stairs and it wasn't long before she brought some coffee up. I sorely wished I had a couple of dollars to give her for the use of the room, but I didn't, so I had to rely on charity. She brought a basin and pitcher to clean myself up with.

"Do you have some clean clothes?" she asked.

I told her I only had what I was wearing. The grip containing the fancy duds I had worn to Doolin's wedding and during holiday with Lucinda had been stolen from the train on the way back from Eureka Springs.

"You look like something the dog rolled in," she said. "I'll see if I can't get you some clothes. Choctaw, strong drink does not agree with your system. You really ought to think about going to a temperance meeting."

I thanked her and said I was through with drinking.

"They all say that the morning after," she said.

I stripped and rolled everything except my leather shirt into a ball to be thrown away. There was no use trying to salvage the trousers, because they were all torn and useless. My leather shirt was in pretty sorry shape as well. You can't wash leather, of course, and it had gotten pretty slick looking in places and there were holes and tears all over. But it had been with me for so long that it felt like a part of me, and I couldn't bring myself to throw it away.

I cleaned my teeth and scrubbed myself nearly raw and washed the mud and leaves out of my hair. The water was pretty black by the time I was done.

Arkansas Tom came up the stairs as I was sitting on the edge of one of the cots, a blanket over me. He was carrying his Winchester in one hand and a package wrapped in brown paper in the other.

"Mrs. Pierce sent this up for you," Tom said. "She sent over to Perry's store for it. There's a bill on top they said you could pay later. What happened to you?"

"Too much forty rod," I said.

"Does it every time," he said. He sat down on the cot next to me. "You know, I'm not feeling well myself. I'm as weak as a cat. I'm afraid I've got the grippe."

He kicked off his boots and stretched out, using his hat to shade his eyes.

I opened the package. There were a pair of trousers and a shirt and a vest, all a sort of medium brown. I put the new clothes on, strapped on my gun belt, and peered at my reflection in the mirror on the washstand.

"What do you think?" I asked Arkansas Tom. He lifted his hat and took me in.

"You look like a store clerk gone bad," he said.

"Well, it will have to do for now," I said.

I brushed as much dirt off my old hat as I could and put it on.

"Tell the boys that I'll be along in a spell," Arkansas Tom said. "They ate breakfast over at Nix's restaurant, and I believe they were headed for the saloon."

At Ransom and Murray's, Doolin was playing poker with my brother Bill, Dynamite Dick, and Tulsa Jack. Bitter Creek was standing with his back to the bar, his boot heel hooked in the brass rail, watching the game.

Red Buck Waightman, who was generally dis-
liked by the gang as a common horse thief, was
away from Ingalls that day and lurking somewhere
down in the Creek Nation. I was hoping he was
stealing me a replacement for Rumbleguts.

The only other customers in the saloon that
morning were Si Newlin, the town drunk, who had
gotten an early start on his career this morning, and
a salesman from Cushing named Walker.

"Where'd you get those duds?" Bitter Creek
asked.

"Don't start," I said. "It was a helluva night."

"Lucky's still giving you trouble," he said. It
was a statement, not a question.

Murray stopped at the poker table, broom in
hand.

"You gents mind if I open the doors?" he
asked. There was a breeze coming up from the Cimarron. "I'd like to air the place out."

"Go ahead," Doolin said, frowning at his cards.

Murray nodded and propped open both the
front and back doors. Old Man Ransom, who
owned the saloon, was asleep on the pool table in
the half-finished shed out the back door, and we
could hear him snoring.

Fresh air washed through the interior of the saloon, cutting somewhat the stench of cigars and
stale beer. From our position at the bar, Bitter Creek
and I could see out the front door all the way down
Second Street to Pickering's Grove.

"More boomers coming in," Bitter Creek com-
mented.

Down at the grove, two big covered wagons
had rumbled in. The wagons were partially hidden
by some outbuildings and a grove of trees.

Si Newlin, who was down at the end of the bar,
quietly passed out. He lost his hold on the bar and

just slid to the ground. Bitter Creek grabbed him by the back of his shirt and dragged him to his usual corner to sleep it off.

"Well, that's all the excitement I can stand for one morning," Bitter Creek said, brushing the sawdust from his hands. "You fellows are about as interesting as paint drying. I'm off to Sadie Comley's to explore the mysteries of the female heart."

"That's not the piece of anatomy that usually interests you," Doolin said.

Bitter Creek laughed and walked through the open front door. His horse was tied at the hitch rail, and Bitter Creek undid the reins and swung up into the saddle. Although Sadie's place was less than a block away, it was a matter of honor for Bitter Creek to ride there instead of walk.

I stood for a moment with my back to the bar, watching what had to be the slowest poker game in the world. My head throbbed and my eyes felt as though somebody had thrown a handful of sand into them. But as bad as I felt physically, it did not compare with the heartache that gripped me when I thought about Lucinda. I decided to follow Bitter Creek to Sadie Comley's. Perhaps I could talk Lucinda into giving us one last try.

I left the saloon and walked north on Ash Street.

Bitter Creek was almost to the corner ahead of me. He was walking his horse and his Winchester was in front of him, across the saddle horn.

Farther down the street, at the Pierce Livery, a man with a rifle had stepped down from a wagon and entered the barn. He was back a moment later, looking up and down the street. Del Simmons was walking toward him from Light's blacksmith shop.

"Who is that rider?" I heard him call to Del.

"Why, that's Bitter Creek!" Del shouted thoughtlessly.

The man—who I now knew was a federal marshal—rested the rifle on the front wheel of his wagon and took aim at Bitter Creek, who was just now drawing up to the town well at the intersection of Ash and Second streets. Before Bitter Creek could raise his gun or turn his horse, the lawman fired.

There was the peculiar whine of lead ricocheting from metal. Bitter Creek stiffened in pain.

The bullet had struck his gun where the tubular magazine joins the receiver, and some of the internal pieces of the Winchester and the shells that it held spilled uselessly out on the ground. The slug had been split in two by its impact with the gun, and while half of it had zinged harmlessly away, the other half had driven deep into Bitter Creek's right thigh and groin. His saddle and right leg were wet with blood.

Bitter Creek managed to fire one shot with the damaged gun, but it went wide of its mark and gouged splinters from the side of the livery barn. Unable to lever a second round, he wheeled his horse to ride for his life.

The lawman stepped clear of the wagon and brought his rifle up for the killing shot.

I drew my revolver.

Without thinking, I fired once, hitting the lawman in the shoulder. Still clutching his rifle, he fell back toward the livery door, then struggled to his feet and tried to make it behind the wagon. Then with cold deliberation I fired again, hitting him square in the chest this time. What I remembered most about killing him is the look of surprise on his face, the horror and disbelief in his brown eyes, and my sudden desperate desire to take the bullet back. His rifle cartwheeled away as he sprawled backward, landing in the dirt with his arms outstretched. From the way he fell, I knew he was dead, or soon would be.

Rifles seemed to erupt from everywhere.

An entire squad of lawmen had invaded Ingalls. I found out later that twenty-three United States marshals and local lawmen had come in the wagons we had seen roll into Pickering's Grove, and in another from the far side of town. The man I had killed was Dick Speed, the city marshal of Perkins.

Del Simmons stood stone still in the middle of the street, horrified by the wounding of Bitter Creek and the killing of the lawman. He looked my way, and on his face was a mixture of disgust and disbelief. Then he sprinted across the street toward the safety of Vaughn's saloon.

A few steps from the doorway, a bullet struck him in the head. He paused in midstep, the hole in his forehead clearly visible. Then he fell in a heap. I could not tell which direction the shot that killed him came from.

Bitter Creek rode past me on his way south. He was slumped in the saddle, his face twisted in pain. "Tell the boys I can do them no good," he said. "I'm bad hurt and have only a farmer's gun to fight with."

I fired the rest of the cartridges in my revolver, spinning first this way and that, trying to give Bitter Creek a little cover to make it out of town.

Bitter Creek dashed into the open door of Ransom's livery, which was next to the Ransom and Murray Saloon. He rode out the rear of the livery and used a deep draw that ran to the southwest for cover.

I ran back toward the saloon, and so many bullets tore into the street around my flying boots that it looked like hail. Strays were zinging everywhere, and a chicken in the middle of the street in front of me was blown apart, feathers flying everywhere. A horse broke loose from the hitch in front of the grocery and ran wildly down the street. It caught a bullet in the spine and went down in a tangle of hooves, unable to move its hind legs. It cried so while on the ground that it would make your heart break just to listen to it.

I dove headfirst into the open doorway of the saloon and kicked the wooden door shut behind me. The door was immediately punctured by a half-dozen bullets, and had I not been lying upon the floor, I would have been killed.

I crawled over to the bar and hunkered down against it while I reloaded. It seemed a damn slow process, flipping open the gate and using the ejector rod to push the spent shells out, one at a time, and then plucking live shells from my gun belt and shoving them into the cylinder, one at a time.

A trio of rounds punched through the front door, about man height. Two of them struck the wall, but one hit the big mirror behind the bar dead center. There are few things as dreadful as the sound of breaking glass, and this broken mirror was the granddaddy of them all. There must have been enough bad luck in that mirror for a lifetime or two. Glass flew everywhere as the mirror disintegrated into slivers of nothingness, and just as it did I saw myself, reflected in a hundred jagged shards—my black hat pushed back on my head, a hard look on my face, and my revolver at the ready. It's strange, but at that moment I thought I saw Bob and Grat, too, but of course, I couldn't have. It must have been Doolin or Dynamite Dick or some of the others.

"Well, son of a bitch," Murray cussed. "Son, you've broken my mirror every damn time you've drawn that gun."

I could have pointed out that I hadn't fired the shot that broke his mirror, but I sort of felt in my bones that he was right.

Doolin and the rest of the gang were clustered around the saloon's back windows, guns drawn, trying to get a shot at the lawmen that were raising so much hell.

Si Newlin was still asleep in his corner.

Walker, the salesman from Cushing, was sitting on his haunches in the middle of the room. His forehead was covered with sweat and his eyes were wild.

When there came a lull in the shooting, Walker got to his feet and stumbled toward the door.

"You'd best wait," Doolin called to him.

"They don't want me," he said. "They want you."

He opened the door and ran outside, screaming for the marshals not to shoot.

A trio of shots came so quickly that they sounded as one.

Walker doubled up and fell into the middle of the street, shot through the liver. He was dying, but it would take some time.

At that moment Old Man Ransom stumbled in through the back door, dragging his leg. The shooting had jarred him awake, and he had run out the back door to see what the commotion was about, and his leg was promptly broke by a rifle shot.

"I'm going to the icehouse boys," the old man said as he made his way to the tiny, sawdust-lined room in the far corner where they kept the ice and liquor. "It's too damn hot out here for me. I think they mean to kill everybody in town."

The marshals moved in, keeping the fire up on all sides of the saloon. We fought back as best we could. Every time Dynamite Dick fired one of his famous cartridges it made a *pop!* and left a black

mark on whatever it hit, but I found no evidence
that it instilled any fear in the hearts of the officers.
There were just too many of them, and they were
shooting the town to pieces. Soon we found ourselves lying on our stomachs as the bullets poked
daylight through the walls and chewed up the inside
of the saloon. Dust, falling from the ceiling, swirled
in the air.

Then the shooting began to slack off, and eventually dribbled to nothing, and the silence turned
out to be almost as bad as the banging away. At any
moment we expected the marshals to come through
the doors or windows as we made a last, desperate
stand. We looked at each other and slowly raised
ourselves off the floor, guns cocked.

"What are they up to?" Dynamite Dick asked.

"I don't know," Doolin said.

Doolin and I crept to a window and dared a
glance over the sill. Among the marshals that were
scurrying from tree to tree and hiding around the
corners of buildings was Lucas—his flaming red hair
and mustache unmistakable.

"They're going for position," Doolin said.
"There's John Hixon from Guthrie. He seems to
be in charge of things. . . . My God, there must be
thirty marshals out there."

Doolin drew back from the window.

"What d'we do?" Tulsa Jack asked. "We'll be
killed."

"We all die someday," Doolin said. "I don't
know about you, but I'd rather die game. Let's give
them one helluva fight if they want to haul our
bloody bodies into Guthrie."

Tulsa Jack didn't look so sure.

Outside, somebody began bellowing Doolin's
name.

I looked over the sill again.

"You, Bill!" It was Hixon. He was standing in the middle of the street, cradling his rifle, waiting for an answer. Dynamite Dick made a move to shoot him, but Doolin knocked away the barrel of his Winchester.

"What do you want, John?" Doolin shouted back.

"Let's chew this thing over a bit," Hixon said. "You're surrounded. You've got to know that you have no chance of escape. Surrender!"

Doolin sucked in his breath. He smoothed the ends of his mustache, then looked at each of our faces. He said in a whisper that he reckoned we were all in agreement.

Then he called back: "Go to hell!"

The firing started again.

"Okay, you can kill him now," Doolin told Dynamite, but of course Hixon had already dove for cover. The barrage this time fairly rocked the old saloon on its foundation.

"Bill, we've got to get out of here," I said.

"Then out the back door to the livery," he said.

Murray appeared at the end of the bar with a rifle.

"You boys have always been straight with me," he said. His hands were shaking. "I reckon the least I can do is provide a little distraction, keep up some fire so they think you're still here."

"You're just what the doctor ordered," Doolin said. "I won't forget this."

"I hope I live long enough to," Murray said, smiling weakly.

"Go to it, barkeep," Doolin told him. Then, to us: "Don't shoot unless they see us."

Murray levered a round and stepped toward the front door. We ran out the back into the unfinished shed. We jumped over the pool table rather than take the time to go around it, and our boots dug some good-sized holes in the green felt. Behind us we could hear Murray firing and the marshals answering with ten shots to his every one.

Doolin led the way out of the shed, followed by my brother Bill and Dynamite Dick. Tulsa Jack and I were the last ones out. Just before I left the shed I heard Murray utter a cry as he was hit. Then we were out in the open and we dashed across to the livery. My bad knee pained me some and for a moment I thought it would go out and leave me on the ground, but it didn't.

The shooting continued, but the marshals didn't know we had fled and they were still concentrating their fire on the saloon.

My brother Bill and I stood guard at the front of the livery stable and Tulsa Jack watched the rear while Doolin and Dynamite Dick saddled and bridled our horses.

One of the marshals had moved up and taken cover behind a big pile of lumber at the corner of Perry's store. From there he had a good view of the livery, and I assumed it wouldn't be long before he and his friends were knocking on our door.

He was just resting the rifle on top of the pile of lumber when he pitched backward, shot through the guts. He dropped his gun and got to his knees, holding his hands around his stomach, and he stumbled toward the street.

"Who fired that shot?" my brother asked.

"It wasn't one of us," I said. "It had to come from down Second Street somewhere. Look! Did you see that?"

Gunsmoke drifted from the roof of the O.K. Hotel.

"My God, it must be Arkansas Tom," I said.

"He's punched a hole in the attic of the hotel and is raining hell down on the marshals."

The lawman had staggered out into the middle of the intersection of Ash and Second, holding his guts in with hands reddened by blood, and he collapsed just a few paces east of the town well. He lay in the road, writhing in pain. We would learn later that his name was Tom Hueston, and he was a constable from Stillwater, and he was indeed potted by Arkansas Tom Jones from his sniper's perch in the attic of Mrs. Pierce's hotel.

"Damn!" Dynamite cursed. "Kid, your lousy horse bit me."

"Isn't there another horse in this livery you can saddle?"

"No, there's just the six."

Doolin smiled.

"Maybe we ought to sic Rumbleguts on the marshals," he said. "That would clear them out in a hurry. I know it would terrify me."

Finally, after what seemed like an eternity, the six horses were ready. We swung up into the saddles and readied our guns for the final battle. Rumbleguts, who was more nervous than usual, tried to nip me on the leg. I smacked him in the jaw, and if I hadn't needed him so badly I would have gotten off and shot him right there.

"Ready? We'll all go out the back," Doolin said.

"No," my brother Bill said. "I think it's better if we split up, with half of us going out the front. Divide their fire."

"You're wrong," Doolin said. "You'll be cut to ribbons because they have the best view of the front of the livery. But I don't have time to argue, so you can suit yourself."

Doolin spurred his horse and burst through the

rear doors of the livery, with Dynamite Dick following. My brother Bill dug his heels into his mount, and Tulsa Jack followed him out the front. I was undecided for a moment. I knew that Doolin was probably right, but I couldn't let my brother ride out the front alone. So I gave a rebel yell and raced after him.

In the split second before I hit daylight, it occurred to me that once again I was the last—the sixth—rider.

It was like riding into a hornet's nest.

Bullets whistled uncomfortably close to my ears as I leaned low over Cimarron's—no, I mean the nag's—mane, wishing I had perfected that Indian trick of hanging on one side of the saddle and shooting beneath the horse's neck. Ash Street looked like those old woodcuts of Civil War battles—dead and wounded men lying about and horses screaming in agony. A blue gunsmoke haze hung over everything and, together with Arkansas Tom's hail of lead from the attic of the O.K. Hotel, provided some cover for our escape.

John Hixon stepped out of the haze at the edge of the street and aimed his revolver dead on at my brother and fired. The slug took Bill's horse in the jaw, and the animal reared and spun uncontrollably, and my brother nearly lost his seat. He got a bit farther down the street and Hixon fired again, this time breaking one of the horse's hind legs. Bill jumped clear as the animal crashed to the ground.

I sent a couple of shots Hixon's way, forcing him to take cover, while Bill grabbed his Winchester and ran. I rode back and met Bill about halfway and helped him up in the saddle behind me, then we tore out after Tulsa Jack.

"Thanks, brother," Bill said.

We had intended to ride down the draw that

cut across the town to the southwest, but when we
got there we discovered our path was blocked by a
wire fence that was too high to jump. The fence was
a long one, and ran between the Ransom and Selph
homes on Third Street. If we tried to go around it
we would become easy targets for the marshals on
either side.

"Who has wire cutters?" Tulsa Jack asked.

I didn't.

Distractedly, I was reloading my Colt while
keeping an eye on a scene to the north of us. One of
the lawmen, pearl-handled revolver drawn, was
struggling to get through the fence to get a shot at
us, but somehow got his coat snagged on the wire
and he pitched backward. I was about to throw
down on him when our ace in the hole, Arkansas
Tom, let him have it. The rifle ball struck the lawman in the chest and came out by his hip.

"Damn," Bill said. "The cutters are in my saddlebags."

"Well, let's do it again," I said, and finished
loading my revolver. "Bill, give me your six-
shooter."

Riding double, we raced Rumbleguts back
down Ash Street to where the wounded horse lay.
Bill slid to the ground while I kept up a steady fire
from the guns in each hand. My horse sidestepped
and capered and nearly bolted, but I managed to
control him long enough for Bill to retrieve the clip-
pers from his saddlebags. Bill sent a round through
the poor beast's head, then he jumped back in the
saddle behind me. Then we rode like hell for a second time down Ash Street to the fence.

The marshal who had caught his coat in the
fence had made his way to the porch of the Ransom
home. He was bleeding badly and was pleading with
Mrs. Ransom to be let in. The old woman refused,

saying she had a pregnant woman in the house that was already scared to death, and that the marshal could just go hide in the cave out back with the children.

I knew him, from Coffeyville. His name was Lafe Shadley and he used to be a deputy sheriff in Montgomery County, Kansas. He was now an Osage Agency policeman at Pawhuska who, like most of the others, had been appointed a special U.S. deputy marshal for the Ingalls raid.

Bill feverishly snipped through the fence and rolled back enough of it to allow us to pass through it into the gulley. The draw was deep, and once inside, we were protected from the barrage of bullets the marshals were sending our way.

We followed the draw as it ran southeast of town. We left it a couple of hundred yards down and mounted a small rise that gave us a view of Ingalls. Shots were still being exchanged between the lawmen and our man at the hotel.

Tulsa Jack pulled his Winchester from his scabbard, swore an oath, and fired a half-dozen shots down Oak Street toward the group of lawmen we could see standing near Doc Pickering's house.

"Which way?" Bill asked behind me.

"I don't know," I said. "It's my guess that Doolin headed south for the Cimarron, maybe crossed over into the Creek Nation."

"I don't care which way we go," Tulsa Jack said, "as long as we *go*."

"Adios, fellows," I said.

I threw my leg over and slid down from the saddle.

"Bill, you can have this sorry excuse for a horse. Get the hell back to your wife and kids and stay there. You were damn lucky today. You can't count on that kind of luck always."

"Where the hell are you going?" he asked.

"There's something I left behind down there," I said.

"What, Arkansas Tom?" Bill snorted. "He can take care of himself."

"No, it ain't him," I said. "But maybe we ought to be thinking of getting him out of there. Now, get out of here. I'll meet up with you later."

"Sam—"

"Go!" I said, and slapped Rumbleguts on the flank. The nag bolted, carrying Bill with it. Tulsa Jack wasted no time in moving out after them.

I began a long walk around the town in order to come back in from the north, where the marshals wouldn't be on the lookout for anybody.

It was near ten o'clock when I walked back into Ingalls and slipped down the alley behind Vaughn's saloon to the back of Sadie Comley's place.

I could see there was still quite a lot of activity around the O.K. Hotel, and I could hear the marshals hollering to Arkansas Tom that they were planning to blast him out with dynamite if he didn't surrender soon. Mrs. Pierce was crying and hollering, and at first I thought she was asking them to spare Arkansas Tom's life, but it eventually became clear that she was pleading with the lawmen not to destroy her hotel.

I eased open the window and stepped up into Lucinda's room.

As I expected, she was still in bed, asleep. She was curled up in a ball, facing away from me. There was a bottle of laudanum on the night table, along with her porcelain teeth which she never wore.

I sat down on the bed and gently touched her arm.

"Darling," I said. "Wake up."

There was no response.

"There's been a lot of shooting today, and I killed a man, but I was lucky—I wasn't hit," I said. "I'm sorry about everything. Let's go away. I can hang up my guns and we can have a normal life, starting right now. I'll clerk in a dry-goods store or sell shoes or grow watermelons, for chrissake—anything, just as long as we're together."

Still, she didn't answer.

"Please, listen to me. Remember what you used to tell me, that where there was life there was hope?"

Impatiently, I tugged at her shoulder.

She rolled toward me.

The sheets were wet with blood.

"Sam," she said weakly. With a great effort she opened her eyes and stared up at me. Her hand sought out mine, and she smiled. "Are we there yet?"

Then she died.

She had been hit in the stomach by one of the stray bullets that had come through the walls. While I had been trading shots with the marshals, she had lain there and slowly bled to death.

The stray could have been fired by the marshals, or it could have been fired by one of the Wild Bunch. It was impossible to tell. Either way, it didn't matter much.

The result was the same.

I scooped Lucinda up and rocked her in my arms. She was light, like a feather, and I was afraid that if I didn't hold her tight she would just float away.

Twenty-one

Doolin and the Wild Bunch escaped.

The King of the Oklahoma Outlaws seemed to vanish, disappearing in the confusion caused by the one hundred thousand homesteaders that had gathered for the impending opening of the Cherokee Strip. The marshals that had laid siege to the outlaw town of Ingalls just days before suddenly found themselves charged with policing a largely drunken mob that had come seeking something for nothing. Civilization, as the newspapers often called it, had come to the Territory in a big way.

The newspapers delighted in reporting the details of the gun battle at Ingalls and its aftermath. Hundreds of rounds had been fired during the fight, and the resulting casualties—three marshals shot dead, two bystanders accidentally killed, and an undetermined number of wounded—left a bloodier mark than any showdown between outlaws and lawmen, including the gunfight at the O.K. Corral.

Evett Dumas Nix, the United States marshal for Oklahoma Territory, swore he would not rest until

the six members of the Wild Bunch who escaped
from Ingalls were brought in, either dead or alive.
He had asked the Justice Department in Washington
for additional men and more money until each of
the outlaws had been tracked down.

Arkansas Tom Jones remained at his sniper's
post in the O.K. Hotel hours after the Wild Bunch
had fled. Despite their threats, the marshals who
laid siege to the hotel had no dynamite with which
to blast him out. Finally, in the middle of the afternoon, low on ammunition and disheartened by the
news that the gang had left him behind, he surren-
dered to U.S. Deputy Marshal Orrington "Red"
Lucas.

He was the only member of the Wild Bunch
captured that day.

Jones—who had been cowboy Roy Daugherty
just weeks before—was placed in a prison wagon
and taken to the territorial jail at Guthrie and
charged with the killings of Speed, Hueston, and
Shadley. The marshals also rounded up nine Ingalls
residents and hauled them in as well, as material
witnesses or on charges of harboring outlaws.

In another wagon was loaded the body of Dick
Speed and the wounded marshals Hueston and
Shadley, and a mad dash was made for the doctors
at Stillwater. Dick Speed was buried the next day at
Stillwater. The others died within the week. Hueston
was buried at Stillwater and Shadley's remains were
sent home to Independence, Kansas. Speed was
twenty-six years old and "had the kindest of dispo-
sitions, was a devoted husband and father, and a
friend of sterling worth."

He left three children.

The newspapers didn't mention his brown eyes.

Bitter Creek escaped to the safety of the Creek
Nation, where his wounds were doctored and

dressed. He was reported to have made a full recovery, and continued his relationship with little Rose Dunn despite the objections of her favorite brother.

Dynamite Dick was shot through the neck during his dash out of Ingalls, but the wound was not believed to be serious. The bandit could, however, be identified by the conspicuous scar which the bullet left.

Walker, the salesman from Cushing, lay in the street until after the battle was over. Then he was picked up and put in a front porch swing until a doctor could be located. He was finally stripped naked and placed behind the glass windows in the front of the Nix Restaurant as part of a treatment to "keep him cool" until he could be taken to Stillwater. He did not survive to make the trip.

Murray the bartender, who wielded a Winchester in an attempt to cover the gang's escape, was shot in the arm and twice in the side, but lived.

Old Man Ransom, whose leg was broken during the gunfight, filed a ten-thousand-dollar suit against the federal marshals for his wound and the damage his saloon building received during the siege. The claim was quickly denied.

The body of Del Simmons was returned to his home at Duncan Bend, Kansas, for burial.

Frank Briggs, an eight-year-old who had been standing close to the marshals on Oak Street when Tulsa Jack fired a barrage from the slope southeast of town, was struck in the shoulder by one of the bullets fired by the outlaw. He survived.

Edith Doolin, who sat out the gun battle in her house on Second Street, was delighted to learn from lawmen the news of her husband's dramatic escape. Mrs. Doolin also reported that she was relieved that her marriage to the outlaw leader had become known to authorities, as she was heavy with child.

And, the papers reported, a prostitute was found dead in a house of ill fame, killed by a stray bullet that was undoubtedly fired by one of the fleeing outlaws. The prostitute was not named. Her body was taken to potter's field, the papers said.

What about the Choctaw Kid?

I was adrift. I wandered the Territory for weeks, nearly out of my head with grief, avoiding any of the places where I would be likely to run into Doolin or the rest of the gang.

Living like some kind of mad hermit, I walked the woods alone, trying to tease some meaning out of life. I was half hoping that I would be cornered by a posse of marshals and forced to wage one final, desperate stand.

I even took to reading the Bible, but I can't say I got any comfort from it. Much of my time with the Good Book was selfishly spent praying for the impossible, as if it were simply a matter of finding the right verse.

The hard truth is that I had lost the one person I loved most, and it was my own fault. If only I had gotten her out of Ingalls before the shooting started, if only I had married her in Eureka Springs when she first suggested it, if only I had *acted* at any one of a dozen different times, Lucinda would have still been alive.

Eventually I drifted north, over the border into Kansas.

I went from town to town, moving steadily northward along the Missouri–Kansas line like some kind of human compass. In time, I reached Kansas City.

I had some idea in the back of my mind that I would visit the orphanage where Lucinda grew up.

Perhaps I could find someone who remembered her, maybe there would be records that could tell me of her real name. Did she still have family living? Would they want to know what became of the daughter that was abandoned in infancy? It would be too much to hope that the nun she admired so much would still be alive. But at least I could stand at the iron fence and watch the people pass by, which would be something to provide a degree of comfort. . . .

On the first Friday in October, with the leaves just beginning to turn and the breeze carrying the promise of winter, I found myself standing on the brick sidewalk on the southwest corner of Seventeenth and Grandview.

The corner was empty of anything except a huge elm tree, twisted and gnarled with age. Its crooked branches towered above me. Around the trunk of the tree was a ring of benches, made from some manner of ornamental iron affair.

I stopped a man in a business coat as he walked by.

"Excuse me, sir," I said. "But could you tell me what happened to the orphanage that was once on this corner?"

"You must have the wrong corner," he said, adjusting his glasses to get a better look at me. "There's never been anything else on this corner, at least not as long as there have been white men here. Why, this corner is sort of a landmark—that elm is two hundred years old."

Twenty-two

The guard ushered me into a windowless gray room that contained one well-worn table and two chairs. He told me to wait and locked the door behind him.

I took a deep breath.

In the guts of the Kansas State Penitentiary at Lansing, with thousands of tons of brick and stone and steel separating you from the outside world, it seems like there isn't enough air to breathe. What air there is smells old and stale, like the kind of air you would imagine trapped inside a tomb. I nudged loose my collar with a finger and placed the camera carefully on the table. I looked at one of the chairs but decided against sitting.

I didn't plan to stay that long.

I closed my eyes and tried to recount every turn and locked door that the guard had taken me through since meeting him at the front gate, but it was impossible.

It wouldn't be enough just to take his keys; it would be necessary to take him hostage as well. He was old and fat, and I didn't expect him to put up much of a fight. Perhaps it was possible to take the warden as well. That, I thought, would be ideal.

Keys jangled and then the door swung open.

Emmett walked uncertainly into the room and sat down when the guard told him to. He was dressed in a gray prison uniform with his number stenciled on the breast. He seemed to have healed well from his wounds and, judging from his fat cheeks, had put on a little weight.

"This here is Emmett Dalton, the only survivor of the raid at Coffeyville," the guard announced. "Emmett, this is—I'm sorry, but what did you say your name was?"

I smiled and held out my hand.

"Tackett," I said.

"Aren't you the photographer who took the nickel postcard of the dead Daltons?" the guard asked. "I thought I met you one day at a photo supply store in Kansas City."

"No," I said. "That's Tackett. I'm Beckett. Thomas Beckett."

"Oh," the guard said, looking puzzled. "I could have sworn you said something else. Now, what magazine are you with?"

"Newspaper," I said. "I'm with the *New York Police Graphic.*"

The guard nodded.

"I think I've seen it," he said.

If he had, it was a miracle, because I had just made it up.

"I'm going to need a little privacy in order to interview Mr. Dalton," I said, taking a pencil and pad from my jacket pocket. "Would you mind waiting outside?"

"Well, we're not supposed to," he said. "But I suppose, since it's Emmett and all, it would be okay.

I'll stand right outside. Is there enough light in here
for you to make a picture?"

The room was lit by a single gas jet with a
green shade that hung over the table.

"Sure," I said, although I really had no idea
how much light it took. "There's always enough
light to shoot by."

"Oh? What kind of exposure are you going to
use?" It was just my luck to get a guard who was an
amateur photographer as well. "It would have to be
pretty long to get anything on film in this light."

"Certainly," I said.

"Then you must be using that new kind of
film?"

"Of course," I said.

The guard nodded knowingly and smiled.

"Well, I knew that you couldn't open the back
of your camera when the warden asked," he said.
"It would ruin your film. Some people just don't understand scientific things, do they?"

"No, they certainly don't."

"Just knock when you're done," he said.

Then he swung the door shut and left us alone.

"Emmett?" I whispered over the table. "Don't
you recognize me? It's Sam, your brother. I'm here
to bust you out."

"Sam?" Emmett asked.

"Yes, it's me," I said. "Damn, it's good to see
you. I vowed that I wouldn't let you rot in prison
for the rest of your life, and I'm here to get you out.
I know that's what Bob would have wanted."

I pulled open the back of the camera.

Tucked inside were two .32-caliber revolvers,
loaded, and a box of cartridges.

"Jesus," Emmett said under his breath. "Are
you trying to get us killed? Shut that up."

Confused, I closed the back of the camera.

"But, Em," I said, "I thought you would want to bust out. We can take your fat guard-friend hostage and shoot our way out if we have to."

"Why would I do a fool thing like that?" he asked. "I've had enough of the outlaw life. As bad as it is in here, it's better than it was *out there*."

"Em, you can't be serious."

"Oh, but I am, little brother," he said. "I'm done with the wrong side of the law. Why, in here I get three squares a day, and a bunk to sleep on, and I'm even learning an honest trade. I'm making clothes."

"Making clothes?"

"Yeah, you know, like a tailor," he said. "And my girlfriend, Julie Johnson, she's waiting for me. They've got to pardon me sometime, don't they?"

"Sure," I said.

"And, you know, I'm kind of a celebrity."

"Great."

Suddenly there didn't seem to be anything to say between us.

"You took a terrible risk coming here," Emmett said. "If they ever found out that you were at Coffeyville, they'd lock you up and throw away the key. Look, I appreciate what you're trying to do, but no thanks."

I nodded my understanding, but I was deflated. How could a Dalton not want to bust out of prison? I had spent weeks planning the escape, finding the right camera, and figuring out what to tell the warden.

"How's the family?" he asked. "I know how Ma is, because I get letters from her, but what about Bill? I read about the shoot-out at Ingalls."

"Bill's okay, I reckon," I said. "At least he got away from Ingalls without carrying any lead. But I'm afraid time is running out for all of us out there.

Everything has changed. The Territory is being settled, and there's an army of lawmen looking everywhere for Doolin and the rest of the Wild Bunch—including somebody with my description."

"There's still time to give up and take your medicine."

"No thanks," I said. "I've seen enough justice for one life. I'll take my chances on the run, just the same."

"Thanks for coming," he said. "But you'd better go. You don't know the risk you're taking."

"Life's a risk," I said, picking up the camera. "The risk I can live with—it's just the regrets that play hell with me. Where there's life, there's hope, is my motto. At least you can't say that your little brother didn't come back for you. Adios."

I knocked on the door.

Emmett was taken back to his cell.

The guard led me back through the maze to the outside, past the gray stone walls and ironwork, and after the gates clanged shut behind me, I stood for a moment in the sunshine.

ABOUT THE AUTHOR

MAX MCCOY is an award-winning journalist and native Kansan. His first novel, *The Sixth Rider,* won the Medicine Pipe Bearer's Award from the Western Writers of America. He teaches fiction at Emporia, Kansas, State University.

Max McCoy is one of today's brightest young writers recounting the legends and spirit of the frontier. His new novel is the sequel to *Sons of Fire*, which was a finalist for novel of the year from the Western Writers of America. In *Home to Texas* we rejoin the Fenns, who are forced from their home by the invading Yankees and must embark on a courageous journey to the Lone Star State.

HOME TO TEXAS

It's the winter of 1863 and the hard-fighting Fenn family leaves their burned-out Missouri home in a stolen Union ambulance wagon for the promise of a better life at the end of the Texas Road. Problem is, brothers Frank and Patrick are both wanted by the Federals for riding with the guerrilla chieftain Quantrill, one of the children becomes desperately sick, and three hundred miles of the bloodiest territory in U.S. history separates them from their dream. While the brothers are handy enough with their revolvers, the real challenge of keeping the family together falls squarely upon their bible-toting wildcat of a sister, Caitlin. But even the Fenns may not be prepared for what fate has in store for them: a cold-blooded Yankee bounty hunter named Thomas Moonlight and his murderous Indian scout, Bone Heart.

Turn the page for a preview of HOME TO TEXAS, a Bantam Domain paperback coming soon wherever Bantam Books are sold.

Prologue

Something's out there."

Joshua Tobias cocked both of the navy revolvers as he drew them from his belt. He nudged the door of the abandoned barn with his shoulder, and the dry leather hinges creaked and gave just enough for him to peer outside.

The moon was new and cast no light, and with the exception of the outline of a partially toppled chimney that marked the spot where a house once stood, the landscape was a dark smudge beneath a canopy of hard bright stars. The night was still, but he could hear no trace of the sound that had inspired his fear—the irregular rasp of something moving cautiously through the hard winter stubble.

Nearby, an owl called.

Far across the barren fields, another owl joined the first in asking the infernal question. Joshua glared at the darkness, daring whatever was out there to show itself.

"I can't see a thing," he said softly, his breath billowing in the cold and frosting his beard. "But I know somethin's out there. It's been following us, John, for three days. I've had a bad feeling ever since we busted caps on that sorry excuse for a dirt farmer."

John Tobias was stretched out on the straw, fully

clothed, with his black slouch hat covering his eyes. The hat—which was his only article of clothing not splattered with red Missouri mud—was badly beaten, but the brim was pinned in front, and a turkey feather was set at a rakish angle on the left side. His hands were folded over the butt of a meticulously clean and loaded .44-caliber revolver.

Beside his brother, beneath a ragged and lice-infested blanket, was a woman.

"Shut the door," John said from beneath the hat. "It's cold."

Joshua carefully eased the hammers down on powder-darkened nipples topped by bright percussion caps and returned the revolvers to his belt. "Maybe we should saddle up," he suggested as he pulled the door shut and set the latch. "Truth to tell, I'd rest easier someplace else. Down by the river, maybe."

In the center of the dirt floor was a lamp improvised from a tin cup of rancid bacon fat, with a rag for a wick. The motion of the closing door caused the flame to undulate and cast grotesque shadows on the rough hewn walls.

Joshua sat cross-legged in front of the light. He picked the cleanest piece of straw he could find within arm's reach and stuck it in the corner of his mouth.

"You'd rest fine here," John said, "if only you'd quit worrying so. Let it go. There's nobody out there. Hell, the Dutch make so much noise they couldn't sneak up on our poor deaf grandmother, and she's been dead for three years."

"Maybe it ain't the Dutch," Joshua said.

John removed his hat.

"I've never known you to be afraid of the Yankees before," he said. "What the hell has gotten into you now?"

"This is something different."

"How?"

Joshua shrugged and thoughtfully chewed the straw.

The woman beside his brother roused and propped herself up on an elbow. The blanket fell away, revealing a swollen breast with a drop of milk gleaming from the tip of a bruised nipple. The woman brushed a tangle of dark hair from her eyes and mumbled a man's name, as if expecting an answer.

"Puddin', go back to sleep," John said replacing the blanket. "Everything's all right."

As the woman groaned and lay back down, Joshua struggled to put into words how close to the animals they had been rendered by the war, how all of their finer emotions had been eclipsed by instinct. Bravery and cowardice were just words; they fought when you had to and ran when they could. There was neither modesty nor shame now, only the alternating fear of death and the thrill of having survived by making others die.

"Rabbits and wolves," he said finally.

"What nonsense are you talking now?" his brother asked, but Joshua couldn't explain it. "You've got yourself good and spooked. Give it up and get some rest. We have to move at first light if we're going to meet up with the boys in the Indian Nations, and I don't want you sleeping in the saddle."

Joshua made a face and spat out the straw.

"We shouldn't have shot the farmer," he said. "I haven't felt bad about anything else we've done, because we done what we had to do, and it was all good and milit'ry. But the farmer was different. He might have been a Yankee sympathizer, but we couldn't prove it . . . John, what if we shot an innocent man?"

"Joshua," his brother said wearily, "there's no such thing."

Joshua sighed. His brother was the elder by two years, and was commonly right about things, but his reassurances did little to ease the knot in his stomach. Joshua blew out the light, and watched as the red ember of the wick struggled against the darkness and lost.

Then he reclined, adjusted the straw beneath his head, and closed his eyes. He silently mouthed the words of a childhood prayer. His right palm was touching the butt of one of the navies, and his index finger rested reassuringly on the cold brass of the trigger guard.

A soft, wet sucking sound brought Joshua Tobias awake. His eyes snapped open and he lay still for a moment, staring upward at a sliver of stars that was visible through a crack in the barn's roof. His heart began to pound like a locomotive.

"John?" he whispered.

There was no reply save for the peculiar coppery smell of fresh blood. He came to his knees, cocked the revolver in his right hand and swung it wildly in the darkness.

"John?" he shrieked.

With his left hand he dug into the breast pocket of his coat, found a match, and struck it with his thumb. The match sputtered and flared, and a piece of the burning head came off under his nail.

He dropped the match.

It took a moment for his brain to register what his eyes had seen in the brief blue flare of the match: a grinning Indian, with greased hair and painted face, holding a hand over his brother's mouth while blood surged from a slit beneath his chin. In the Indian's hand was a curved skinning knife. His brother's eyes were wide and pleading as rose-colored bubbles bloomed from his neck.

Before the match hit the ground, and just as his finger began to tighten on the trigger, Joshua found himself driven forward as if kicked by a mule. His revolver spat its ball harmlessly into the roof. He landed on his face in the dirt and dried manure of the barn floor, his ears ringing, a peculiar warmth spreading across his back.

Someone lit the tin cup of bacon grease.

The barn was filled with smoke and the sulfurous stench of black powder. The navy had fallen half a yard away, and Joshua's fingers groped for it. A boot came down upon his hand, but Joshua didn't have the strength to cry out.

"Where is Quantrill?"

With the boot still firmly in place, Captain Thomas Moonlight knelt. He had a long tanned face that made his blue eyes seem even paler, and a finely trimmed mustache that resembled cornsilk. He removed his hat, then pulled off his gloves.

"How old are you, son?" he asked.

"Eighteen," Joshua managed.

"Damned young to die," the captain said evenly. "But you've taken a pistol ball square in the spine. Can you move your legs? No, I reckoned not."

Joshua turned his head toward his brother, who now appeared quite dead. The Indian was at work with the skinning knife, laying bare the white bone beneath the scalp. The woman was huddled against the wall, the blanket pulled tightly over her head.

"Quite a savage, isn't he?" Moonlight asked. "But a brother, nonetheless. *For he today that sheds his blood with me shall be my brother; be he ne'er so vile, this day shall gentle his condition.*"

There was a wet sliding sound that reminded Joshua of skinning rabbits as the Indian pulled his brother's scalp free of the skull. Joshua choked back a column of bile that rose volcanically in his throat.

"Now," Moonlight said. "If you don't want Bone Heart to lift your hair also, you'll tell me where that devil Quantrill is and what he's up to. Hurry, for you don't have much time left."

Joshua swallowed and closed his eyes.

"Bound for Texas."

"Where is he now?"

"Don't know," Joshua said and licked his lips. "The boys scattered after the fight at Baxter Springs.

The colonel told us to rendezvous in the Nations and beat a path down the Texas Road to the Red River."

Moonlight frowned.

"I could guess that much," he said. "I want to know where Quantrill is *now.*"

"I have no idea where the colonel might be."

"He doesn't deserve the title," Moonlight said. "My tracker Bone Heart has more basic decency than the infamous Quantrill. At least the Osage religion condones the murder, rape, and robbery of one's enemies."

Joshua's eyes narrowed with guilt.

"Who's the woman?" Moonlight asked. "One of Quantrill's whores?"

"Ain't no whore," Joshua said. "Found her in the woods, more than half crazy and crying about her dead kid. Never could get a name out of her. We was going to leave her with the first family we came to, but we never found none. Everybody's gone."

Joshua began to cough.

"I'll see that she's taken care of," Moonlight said.

"Yankees seem to have a peculiar way of taking care of people," Joshua said and smiled. Blood etched the spaces between his teeth.

Moonlight drew the .44-caliber Remington revolver from its holster for the second time that night. He laid the muzzle squarely against the back of Joshua's head, which was turned to face his dead brother.

"*Go thou,*" Moonlight said as he squeezed the trigger, "*and fill another room in hell.*"

One

The sun was a tarnished disk behind a blanket of scalloped clouds on the western horizon, casting a weak light that robbed the prairie of its color. Shadows pooled and spread like the rising of an inland sea, a relentless tide of muted blues and grays that blotted up the terrain.

Even the air seemed dead to the concerns of men. There was no wind, and sounds were curiously muffled in the unnatural stillness. Conversations became a sleep-inducing drone, and distant gunshots were but the popping of trees in winter.

The little Rucker ambulance wagon, with its green sides and bright red wheels, seemed to be the only bit of life on this soundless and monochromatic landscape. It bumped and clattered over the prairie, the USA that was proclaimed in bold black letters on its canopied sides shook, and its hubs howled for grease. The unruly team that pulled the wagon often attempted to go two directions at once, snapped at one another with bared teeth, and left steaming piles of horse apples that marked the trail.

Patrick Fenn rode ahead of the wagon, his collar turned against the October chill, his coat hiding a mismatched pair of revolvers in his belt. Although his eyes tung, he remained alert, always scanning the terrain a undred yards distant.

For hours they had passed nothing but blackened himneys that stood like unlettered monuments to the var that had devastated the border between the old lave-holding state of Missouri and the new free-soil tate of Kansas. Their flight from Cass County had een unchecked; the border had become a sort of pur- atory on earth, devoid of fences or domesticated ani- nals or human beings in residence.

Patrick Fenn heard the axle break as one of the ront wheels came up hard against a boulder hidden by clump of dead grass. He turned his horse in time to ee the iron-rimmed wheel snap free of the linchpin nd bounce away. The front corner of the ambulance ilted earthward, spilling his sister Caitlin and her bible nto the ground.

Frank Fenn rode the dashboard like a sailor fight- ng a heavy sea as the broken axle dug into the earth, ocking the front wheel at an awkward angle that hreatened to overturn the little wagon. Frank wrapped he reins around both fists and put his back against the eam, but the confused horses continued to struggle gainst the unnatural drag behind them. The rear vheel opposite the broken axle began to lift.

Patrick jumped from the saddle, stumbled for a ew steps, then rushed to the team. He grabbed the bri- lle of the nearest horse and planted his feet. His boots kidded over the cold ground, and he watched the rear vheel as it spun lazily above the ground. The horses topped and then shuffled backward a bit, and the am- ulance came to rest, rocking heavily on its springs.

"Who's hurt?" Frank called.

"Little Frank's got a bump on his head the size of walnut," Patrick, who had already lifted the canvas nd was taking a quick census, said. "Jenny's got a cratch on her forehead. Trudy was holding Annabel, nd they both seem fit enough."

Patrick retrieved the big bible from the ground and helped Caitlin to her feet. She hopped unsteadily to the wagon and glared at Frank. "I've only got one leg left," she said, shaking with anger. "Do you think I want to snap it off and spend the rest of my life scooting along the ground like some kind of two-legged dog?"

Tight-lipped, Frank jumped down.

"All this family has left in the world is each other and this sorry Yankee idea of a wagon," Caitlin went on. "If Pa were alive, he'd knock some sense into your head. I reckon you learned to drive a team from one of those books you read back east. Did you learn how to fix axles, too?"

"It was an accident," Jenny said protectively as she climbed down from the wagon, Little Frank on her hip. "Let's not start blaming each other for things. It's done, and the question now is how to fix things."

"The axle's busted clean in two," Patrick said, squatting for a better look. "We're going to need a good-size timber to replace it, at least as thick as your leg."

"Where's the closest stand of wood?" Caitlin asked.

"Drywood Creek, most likely," Patrick said. "Three or four miles to the south. I reckon it will take the rest of the day to find the right tree, hack our piece out, and bring it back."

"Then how long will it take to fix?"

Patrick withdrew an ax from the back of the ambulance.

"Another day at least," he said, testing the blade of his ax with his thumb. "And that's reckoning that the wheel can be straightened enough to use. You might as well make camp here as best you can."

"Two days," Frank said. "In two days we could have been in the Indian Nations."

"Then we'll be there in four," Patrick said.

"Give me the ax," Frank said. "I'll go for the timber."

"Frank, you'd better stay with the wagon," Patrick said as he swung up in the saddle. "I'm sure you can do this as quick as I can, but I reckon Jenny would feel better having you here."

"We'll need some food," Frank said. "All the farms have been picked clean for miles around, but we might be lucky enough to find a squirrel or a rabbit that somebody else missed."

Patrick pulled his one good revolver from beneath his coat and handed it to the Indian girl. It was a Colt, .36-caliber, with a fully capped and loaded cylinder. The one he kept in his belt was a Joslyn that could carry only four rounds, since two of the chambers were cracked.

"Let Trudy hunt," he said. "I know she's good at it."

Trudy nodded and took the gun.

"Well," Caitlin said. "That's the plan. The rest of us should start gathering whatever we can find that will burn. It's going to be cold tonight, and judging from those clouds on the horizon we're going to have an early snow."

Patrick self-consciously gave Trudy a smile and winked at his sister. Then he walked his horse a few yards away from the others, and motioned for a word with his older brother. Frank held the bridle while Patrick spoke softly enough so that the others couldn't hear.

"If I'm not back tomorrow, mount them double on the team and get them out of here," Patrick said. "This is a dismal place—you'll freeze or starve to death if a Yankee patrol doesn't catch you first. They need you with them, not swinging at the end of a rope."

TWO

Snowflakes swirled out of the darkness as Thomas Moonlight dismounted at the field headquarters of General James G. Blunt, Union commander of the District of the Frontier. Moonlight handed the reins to one of Blunt's troopers and ordered him to treat Calaban as gently as a rich widow.

Moonlight paused at the entrance to Blunt's tent and smoothed his hair and mustache before announcing himself. Then one of the general's senior bodyguards parted the flap and escorted Moonlight inside.

Blunt was seated at his field desk. He looked up from his reports and studied Moonlight, then asked the sergeant to leave them. The general was a short man with dark hair and a swarthy complexion, and he seemed self-conscious in front of this near-albino giant. Blunt lit a cigar, then offered one to Moonlight, who refused.

"Report," Blunt said, smoke curling from the corners of his mouth. Moonlight withdrew a sheaf of blood-stained papers and placed it on the general's desk.

"Loyalty oaths, sir," Moonlight said. "Some of the partisans had two or three on them, each swearing allegiance to the Union. Those account for thirteen of Quantrill's men."

Blunt poured a snifter of brandy from a bottle on his desk, then took a long drink, as if girding himself for the next question.

"What of Quantrill?" he asked.

"In hiding," Moonlight said. "Waiting to rendezvous in the Nations and lead his men to the Red River. He will soon be out of our reach."

"Damn him," Blunt said, rubbing his jaw. "The fool thought he'd killed me at Baxter Springs. If he'd left any prisoners alive he would have learned that they'd killed Major Curtis instead."

Two weeks earlier—Oct. 6, 1863—Quantrill had chanced upon upon a wagon train of Blunt and a hundred of his men just outside of Baxter Springs, Kansas, above the Indian Nations. Blunt had mistaken Quantrill's line of ambiguously-clad raiders as an honor guard sent to greet him from the Union outpost at Baxter Springs, and the mistake had nearly proved fatal. In addition to killing seventy-nine of Blunt's men, the guerrilla chieftain also captured all of the general's correspondence, his commissions, two stands of colors, and the general's own sword. Blunt himself had only narrowly escaped capture, by running wildly in fear of his life.

"Begging the general's pardon," Moonlight said, as the general appeared lost in thoughts of his own. Moonlight poured himself a shot of brandy. "I await your orders, sir."

"Orders?" Blunt asked. "I want Quantrill. I want him to pay for the murder of my men . . . and of my reputation."

Moonlight smiled knowingly.

"Until I have Quantrill," Blunt continued, "I want you to hunt down as many of the men who participated in the burning of Lawrence and in the massacre at Baxter Springs as you can. No quarter, captain."

"*Cry havoc,*" Moonlight recited, "*and let slip the dogs of war.*"

"Your tactics have worked well thus far," Blunt said admiringly. "That red Indian of yours—bless his murderous soul—has proved more effective at bringing these traitors to task than anyone expected."

"Thank you, sir," Moonlight said. "It *is* a different war here on the frontier. One has to think—and to fight—differently in order to be successful."

"You are correct about fighting differently, of course," the general said. "Tell me, captain, what besides their intimate knowledge of the country and their secret network of support make the guerrillas most effective?"

"Their hatred of us," Moonlight said. "Their uncommon courage. Horsemanship. And, of course, the fact that we have placed them in a position of fighting to the death."

"No, no," Blunt said, waving Moonlight's comments aside. "Think in terms of firepower."

"Ah," Moonlight said. "Their revolving pistols. With each partisan carrying at least two, they can get off twelve shots in the time it takes one of our regulars to fire his rifle and reload."

"Precisely," Blunt said. "The solution, I believe, is to have a squad of our own—your squad, Moonlight—armed with a weapon that is superior even to a brace of revolving pistols. Open the crate on the ground behind you, captain."

Moonlight knelt and removed the lid to a wooden box that resembled something more like a coffin than a shipping crate. From it he removed a lever-action rifle with a brass receiver, one of a dozen tucked inside.

"Henry's Volcanic repeating rifle," Blunt said.

"I've read of them," Moonlight said.

"The tubular magazine beneath the barrel holds sixteen brass-cased rimfire cartridges, and you can shoot them all as fast as you can work the action," Blunt said. "Forty-four caliber, with a practical range of four hundred yards."

"Surely not," Moonlight said. He shouldered the weapon, sighting down the long octagonal barrel at an imaginary point on the tent wall. He could feel the weapon as an extension of himself, of his will.

"You be the judge," Blunt said. "You may have six of the rifles, and two hundred rounds for each of your men. The remaining six are for my bodyguards."

Moonlight lowered the rifle.

"These weapons come dearly," Blunt said. "More than forty dollars each. If one of your troopers falls, see that the rifle is recovered. And don't give one to that red Indian."

"Of course not."

"Look here, Moonlight," Blunt said. He stood now, and came around the desk and stood so close that Moonlight could count the pores on the general's nose. "You may take any means necessary to accomplish your objective. You may use your own discretion and I expect to have no further discussion regarding this directive, which will remain implicit between you and me. You are to report in a month's time. Understood?"

"Understood, sir."

"Also," Blunt said, picking through the papers on his desk. "I want you to be particularly watchful for a deserter and his brother who were participants at Baxter Springs. Odd, but reports indicate they made off with my Rucker ambulance wagon."

Blunt handed a report to Moonlight.

"The deserter's name is Frank Fenn. He was an officer with Halleck's command at St. Louis before he turned coat and joined his secessionist brothers on the border. One of the brothers was captured and hanged, but the other is still causing a good deal of trouble."

"Yes, sir."

"I hate deserters, Moonlight," Blunt said. "I want you to place this Frank Fenn and his surviving brother just a little lower on your list than the prince of darkness himself."

"Sir," Moonlight said.

Blunt saluted, and Moonlight came to attention and returned the gesture, waiting to be dismissed. But the general paused, then placed a hand on Moonlight's shoulder.

"Captain," he said, "bring my god-damned sword back."